OLAF OLAFSSON

Valentines

Olaf Olafsson was born in Reykjavik, Iceland, in 1962. He studied physics as a Wien Scholar at Brandeis University. He is the author of three previous novels, *The Journey Home*, *Absolution*, and *Walking into the Night*. He lives in New York City with his wife and three children.

Valentines

Valentines

stories

OLAF OLAFSSON

ANCHOR BOOKS
A Division of Random House, Inc.
New York

Many thanks to Victoria Cribb
for her invaluable assistance when writing this book.

"April" originally appeared in *Zoetrope: All-Story* in December 2006.

The Library of Congress has cataloged the Pantheon edition as follows:
Ólafur Jóhann Ólafsson.
Valentines : stories / Olaf Olafsson.
p. cm.
I. Title.
PS3615.L34V35 2007
839'.6934—dc22
2006025508

Anchor ISBN: 978-0-307-28055-8

Book design by Soonyoung Kwon

www.anchorbooks.com

Printed in the United States of America
10 9 8 7 6 5 4 3 2 1

Valentines

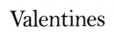

january

He had suspected he might have to spend the night in New York. The plane had left an hour late from Iceland and circled for a long time over Kennedy Airport before getting permission to land. The pilot had said there were problems on the ground with ice and strong crosswinds, and for a while it looked as if they would have to land somewhere else. But at last he began the descent, the flight attendants took their seats and those who were afraid said their prayers, promising to lead better lives in future.

Tomas, a seasoned traveler, wasn't worried. He knew there wouldn't be any flights to Chicago till the following day so he decided to go into Manhattan and spend the evening there. He liked the city and often traveled there on business, particularly when he was younger. Once there had been talk of his being transferred there, the time when Ira Taubman and Harry Poindexter decided to retire and the company worried they would lose contact with important clients on the East Coast. But the old men had prepared the ground for Tomas and their other successors and the transition was smooth. This was a relief to everyone but it gave Tomas pause for thought because the old men had always been considered indispensable. He had blurted this out to Taubman when they ran into each other at the sauna some months later, and the old man slapped him on the back with an indulgent smile and said: "No one's indispensable in business, Tomas my boy. Not even you." Having already concluded this himself, Tomas was able to join in his laughter. Taubman had always been his model, easygoing and levelheaded, never pressuring his clients. Tomas had learned from him not to push shares that he wouldn't buy himself or chase short-term profits. Taubman and Poindexter had earned respect. They phoned their clients every day, knew the names of their wives and kids, even what car they drove. Although he never got himself a computer, Taubman always had an answer ready and his desk was impeccably tidy. When the market took a dive he was the one everyone called. He kept his head, neither buying nor selling till the volatility was over. A bachelor like Tomas, he was always meticulously dressed, even after he retired. He had introduced Tomas to his tailor, a painstaking, reasonably priced man who never forgot to praise Tomas for not putting on weight.

Tomas's father had been American, his mother Icelandic. He grew up in Chicago, an only child, but moved to Iceland with his mother after his father died. He was a teenager at the time. They rented an apartment by the harbor and his mother got a job in the claims department of an insurance company. Tomas finished high school in Reykjavík but went back to the States to attend university, first Chicago State, then Northwestern. He hadn't been unhappy in Iceland, but he never put down roots there, missing his old home by Lake Michigan.

In recent years Tomas had made it a rule to go to Iceland for New Year's. He generally arrived on the twenty-seventh or twenty-eighth of December and left on January second. His mother lived in an old people's home but was still joyful and energetic. He would meet friends and relatives, inviting up to a dozen people to dinner at the Grill or Hotel Holt on New Year's Eve. His mother looked forward to this evening all year. She was always in great form and before the night was over she never missed a chance to ask her son when he was going to get married. He usually smiled, took her hand and said: "Who knows, Mom?" because he didn't want to disappoint her.

But this time the question made him stop and think. He had known it was coming yet still found himself lost for words. Recently he had been wondering whether he would always be alone. He was not young anymore and had recently begun to suffer from a sense of discontent that had never plagued him before. He had been jolted just before Christmas when he visited Taubman and the old man told him: "I talked to Maureen the other day. She asked about you. She's now living in New York."

He had only once been in what people call a serious relationship. That was ten years ago when he lived with Maureen. She was several years younger than he and worked in advertising. They had met at Taubman's seventieth birthday and walked together into the garden of the hotel where the party was being held. There they sat on a bench under a tree and talked. It was late but still warm, the lights aglow among the flowers and shrubs and a cheerful din coming from the hotel. She moved closer to him without any apparent design and her laugh was bright and artless. She was wearing a white backless dress and he gazed at her long, slender neck and her shoulders, which were so delicate that he wanted to touch them out of simple curiosity. He called her at work several days later and invited her to dinner. She accepted gratefully and her voice sounded as bright and genuine over the phone as when they had sat in the garden. Two months later she moved in with him. Although it had been his suggestion, he was not prepared. He was set in his ways, never having had to worry about anyone but himself since he had left home. His life was neat and orderly; his days were all the same.

He was in the office by half past seven on weekdays and woke early on weekends, read the papers, tidied up, took a walk around his neighborhood or visited galleries before going to the sauna that he and Taubman frequented. On Saturday evenings he dined with friends. He lived a simple life, taking care to have a routine for everything and avoid upsets.

He had always tried to keep his feelings on a tight rein. His psychologist traced this to his father's death. They had been very close and when his father had passed away he had silently blamed his mother for not grieving enough. Tomas mentioned this to his psychologist once he began to trust him. They discussed the past at length and eventually concluded that it had been out of care for Tomas that his mother had never broken down in his presence. He regretted having judged her, even if only in thought.

He had difficulty adapting to the change of routine, and Maureen assumed that he felt she was in his way. She wasn't demanding but sensitive and every now and then felt the need to tell him how much she loved him. He, on the other hand, did not make unprompted declarations; it was not his way.

When he felt he was finally growing used to living with her, she broke off their relationship. They had then lived together for more than a year and he had begun to enjoy waking up before her and watching her sleep. But he never told her that and refrained from touching her while she slept. He felt lucky to have met her and expected a happy future. He was speechless when she said it would probably be best for them to go their separate ways.

"I don't think you love me," she said.

He was about to try to convince her that she was wrong and ask her to stay but abandoned the attempt. He thought that maybe his love wasn't adequate, maybe there were others who were capable of loving more passionately. It wouldn't be fair for him to get in her way. He imagined that she had already met someone who was better for her but couldn't bring herself to tell him.

He helped her move and called her regularly for the next few weeks to hear how she was doing. Perhaps she felt he was nursing her as if she were one of his clients, but she talked to him anyway and tried to sound cheerful. Then she asked him to stop calling.

"You needn't worry about me," she said. "I'm going on vacation and when I come back I'm starting a new life."

They hadn't met since. Apart from hearing that she'd moved to Europe he had lost touch with her. So had Taubman, and Tomas had stopped asking him about her. He hadn't forgotten her, though, and once in Paris he caught himself looking for her. He found this strange, as he had no idea where in Europe she lived. But he could picture her in a city like Paris with her long, slender neck and those birdlike shoulders. Paris or Rome or Florence. That's where shoulders like those belonged.

After that he had been wary in his dealings with women, taking care not to rush into anything. His relationships didn't last long. The women wanted a commitment.

From the airport, Tomas booked a hotel room while waiting for his baggage. He knew the Plaza Hotel was now closed so he tried elsewhere. He liked the old hotels best, where the furnishings were heavy and venerable and time seemed to stand still. Of course he could have spared himself the journey into the city and taken a room at one of the airport hotels, but he knew he wouldn't feel at ease there. Once he had caught the flu and been stuck in an airport hotel in Seattle and the memory still haunted him. The room had been bare, the lighting cold, and all that he could see from the window were a parking lot, a freeway and a warehouse with the logo of a foreign airline. He could still remember the emptiness and silence in the middle of the day, the dirty carpet, the foul-tasting tap water. Overwhelmed by a sense of dread he had checked out, even though he was still running a high fever. It had taken him longer to shake off the dread than the flu.

There was a long wait for the baggage. His thoughts went to Maureen while bags from an earlier flight wound their way past. He had been thinking of her on the plane and after landing, when it became clear that he wouldn't make it to Chicago that night. "She asked about you," Taubman had said. "She's now living in New York."

He loathed being forward. He never cold-called prospective clients, preferring instead to let middlemen make initial contact. But she had asked about him and fate was leading him to the city. Finally he decided to take a chance and called directory assistance.

Maureen Egan. There were two by that name, one on East Seventy-fifth, the other in SoHo. He thought it more likely that she would live on the Upper East Side and quickly tapped the number into his phone so he wouldn't forget it. Yet he didn't call her right away, feeling he needed to give it more thought. It had been such a long time. Ten years. But she had asked after him, and although he hadn't pressed Taubman for any more information he had sensed from the old man that she had asked out of interest. "Apparently she's single again," he had said.

He didn't call until he was in the taxi. It was snowing and traffic was moving slowly.

"Hello."

"Maureen?"

"One moment."

He almost hung up but stopped himself. When she finally came to the phone he recognized her voice immediately.

"Maureen?"

"Yes?"

"Tomas Eliot."

"Tomas? I can't believe it."

"I'm sorry to bother you."

"You're not bothering me."

"Taubman told me you were living in New York."

"Where are you? It's a bad connection."

"I'm in a taxi on my way into the city. I was wondering if we could meet."

"Meet?"

"I understand if you can't. I just thought it would be good to hear your voice. Taubman told me you were living here now."

"Yes, I moved."

"I understand if you're busy. I shouldn't have bothered you."

"No, we should meet."

"I was going to fly to Chicago tonight but they've canceled all the flights. Are you free tomorrow morning?"

She didn't answer immediately.

"I can't do tomorrow morning," she said then.

"I understand. Perhaps we could just meet next time I'm in town."

"Where are you staying?"

He told her.

"That's not far from here. I could stop by."

"Are you sure that's not an inconvenience? With the weather . . ."

"What did Ira tell you?"

"He said you'd asked about me."

There was a silence, and Tomas was about to repeat that they could just meet another time when she cleared her throat and said: "I'll come by around ten-fifteen."

He was in Manhattan just after nine. The hotel was in the Sixties, between Madison and Fifth. He was greeted warmly and the lighting in the lobby was dim and cozy. His room faced the street, and the porter who carried up his luggage for him said that things had been very busy over the holidays but were now quieting down. There were cut flowers in a vase on the coffee table and chocolates on the pillow. Tomas ran himself a bath.

At ten he went downstairs. He had reserved a table in the library next to the bar where you could have your meals brought to you as you sat in the deep, comfortable armchairs. A fire was burning in the hearth, its warmth reaching out to him and the flames casting a glow on the wood-paneled walls.

Feeling good after his bath, a change of clothes and a slap of aftershave on his cheeks, he decided to have a drink. He savored it slowly while studying the menu the waiter had placed on his table. Maureen. After all these years. Would she have changed? Would she still be as genuine and warm? As . . .

He didn't finish the thought. She was in the doorway when he looked up, wearing a warm coat. She looked the other way so at first he wasn't sure it was her. But when she moved her head his heart leaped and he hurried over to her.

"Maureen," he said.

"Tomas."

"It's so good to see you."

They smiled. Not sure whether to shake her hand or kiss her, he did neither.

"It's so good to see you," he repeated. "How long has it been?"

"Ten years," she said.

"Ten years," he repeated as if taken aback. "Are you sure?"

"Yes," she said. "It's ten years."

He helped her out of her coat and handed it to the waiter. They went into the library, she leading the way. She had always been slim, but he thought she had lost weight. Yet she looked good, her face smooth and her eyes clear, though perhaps she seemed a little tired. The veins in her neck that he had stroked so often were still faintly traced.

They had never quarreled. She had never blamed him for anything, not even toward the end when he had stopped stroking her neck. Not in the morning when he found her crying in the bathroom but couldn't think of any words of comfort. Never.

He studied her now as if to confirm that she was real and not a figment of his imagination. She was wearing dark trousers and a green pullover with a red stone on a silver chain. She hadn't grayed.

"Well," he said. "After all these years."

"Yes," she said. "All these years."

"You look well."

She stared at him as if she hadn't heard what he said, then replied: "You were always so polite."

The waiter came over and asked what he could get them. Tomas told her he hadn't eaten yet and asked whether she'd have something to keep him company. She said she wasn't hungry. He asked if she'd like a dessert. She declined but asked the waiter to bring her herbal tea. Tomas ordered a light supper and a soda water.

"I've just flown in from Iceland," he said.

"Really?" she said. "Is your mother still alive?"

"Yes," he said. "She's in good spirits. Like most people her age she has become a bit forgetful but mostly about things she doesn't want to remember."

She smiled the same smile as before. It was friendly yet somehow different from how he remembered.

"It would be good if we could all do that."

There was no trace of bitterness in her words so he smiled and agreed with her.

"Yes," he said, "it would help."

He studied her. She looked around, clasping her fingers, then loosening them again, brushing a lock of hair behind her ear. She wasn't wearing a wedding ring.

"You haven't changed at all," he said, adding in explanation when he realized how threadbare those words sounded on their own: "You still have the same gestures."

"Really?" she asked.

"Brushing your hair behind your ear."

"Did I do that?"

The waiter brought the tea and soda water, placing them on the table between them.

"Milk?" he asked. "Sugar?"

She declined.

"You always used to brush your hair behind your ear," said Tomas. "Your right ear. You even did it the evening we first met."

"At Ira's birthday," she added.

"Yes, when we sat out in the garden and you said you had danced too much."

"Did I say that?"

"You were wearing new shoes. They were pinching."

"You remember that."

"They've closed down the hotel."

"What was it called again?"

"The Drake."

"Yes, the Drake. It's such a long time since I've visited Chicago."

"It's an office building now."

"Really?"

"Yes, there have been a lot of changes over the last few years."

As she drank her tea he watched her raise the cup to her lips and set it down again.

"You moved to Europe, I was told."

"Did Ira tell you?"

"Yes, he did. Were you there long?"

"Eight years. I came home two years ago."

"And since then?"

"Here and there. What about you?"

He smiled.

"Always in the same place. Every day like the last. I get more set in my ways by the year. Sometimes I wonder what would happen if I packed up and moved away. Began a new life."

"Where?"

"I don't know. Paris . . . Florence . . . Burma . . ."

He laughed at himself.

"Such nonsense. I shouldn't be telling you this. You'll think I've lost my mind."

"I'm sure lots of people think like that," she said.

"Once I dreamed I'd moved to Buenos Aires and changed my name so I couldn't be traced. When I woke up I realized what nonsense it was. Just who did I think would come looking for me?"

He laughed and she smiled and drank her tea. The waiter brought the food, a chicken sandwich and salad.

"I hope you don't mind my having a bite to eat," he said.

"Bon appétit."

"I suppose you're still into all that health food?"

She stirred the teaspoon around her cup, first clockwise, then counterclockwise.

"Yes, I guess so," she said, adding: "Did you never marry?"

"No," he said. "You?"

"I was married for several years. We divorced."

"Was that in Europe?"

"Yes, in Italy."

"You didn't live in Rome?"

"No."

"Florence?"

"No," she said. "Why did you think that?"

"I don't know," he said. "Just a guess."

"We lived in Milan."

He nodded. She looked into the fire.

"Did you have children?"

"No."

She clasped her fingers and looked over at the door.

"I hope I'm not keeping you," he said.

"It was just the sound of the wind," she said. "It's quite a storm."

"The flights have all been canceled," he said.

The evening before Maureen moved out he had made up a bed for himself on the sofa in the living room. It hadn't happened before, but that evening he felt it was the right thing to do. He had expected her to be secretly relieved, so he was taken aback by her reaction.

"Why?" she asked. She was so upset that he was shocked. He moved back into the bedroom for that night, putting his arms around her when she cuddled up to him but taking care to stop there. He had also restrained himself in the morning when he had been on the verge of asking her to stay. It hadn't been easy, but she didn't deserve to be confused. He couldn't do that to her.

The waiter took away the plate and cutlery. The fire was still burning but the staff had stopped feeding it, as it was getting late.

"Maureen," he said, taking a deep breath. "Maureen, I often think about you. I hope you don't mind."

She looked away.

"I sometimes wonder what would have happened if we hadn't . . . gone our separate ways. I wonder what life would have been like."

She didn't answer.

"Perhaps I have no right to say this after ten years. But we all grow up eventually. We better understand what matters. And realize what's gone wrong."

She was silent. He lowered his eyes.

"I'm sorry," he said. "I shouldn't have said that."

He looked at her.

"I'm sorry," he repeated.

"What did Ira tell you?"

"Pardon?"

"He promised me. . . . I don't want your pity, Tomas. I never wanted that."

"You mustn't think I pity you, Maureen. My feelings . . ."

"You were always good to me, Tomas."

"It wasn't out of pity."

"Let's be honest with each other. It was for the same reason you got in touch this evening. Things look better than when I spoke to Ira. The doctors are optimistic. You can't imagine how great they are."

He was shocked. When she saw his face she seemed suddenly unsure.

"Maureen," he said, "what's wrong?"

"Nothing," she said quickly. "Nothing the doctors can't handle. When I spoke to Ira . . ."

She clasped and unclasped her fingers faster than before. He noticed her hands were shaking.

"Maureen."

"I don't want to talk about it," she said. "I don't want you to pity me."

They sat in silence; she looked away.

"Who answered the phone when I called?" he asked.

"My sister."

"Is she staying with you long?"

She didn't answer.

"I was relieved when you called," she said. "I'd been meaning to get in touch with you for so long. But I didn't have the nerve."

"Why not?"

"I was pregnant when I left you. I knew a week before I moved out."

He didn't know what to say. Her words seemed to come from a great distance.

"I carried the baby as long as I could," she continued, "because I didn't know what to do. Once I was about to tell you but someone came into your office and you had to hang up. It was raining that day."

He reached for the water but put it down without drinking.

They were silent, both staring into space. The fire was dying in the hearth, but the embers still cast a faint glow on the floor.

"Why didn't you tell me?" he almost asked but didn't. There was no point.

"I'm sorry," she whispered.

He looked down, trying to gather his thoughts.

"I'm glad you called," she said then. "I always feel happy when I think of you."

"What can I do for you?" he asked.

"Nothing," she said. "You don't need to do anything for me."

They both heard the wind. Somewhere a door slammed.

"Well," she said. "It's late."

He nodded.

She stood up, hesitating a moment before putting her arms around him and giving him a quick hug and kiss on the cheek.

"I'm glad we met this evening," she said.

They were the only ones left and the waiter was quick to bring her coat. Tomas helped her into it, then they left. A couple entering the hotel stopped in the lobby to shake off the snow before walking to the elevators.

"I hope I'll be able to get a taxi," she said.

"I'll ask the doorman."

Tomas went out to the sidewalk. It was cold and windy. The doorman said there might be a wait. Tomas breathed the cold air before going back inside.

"Maureen," he said, "can we meet tomorrow?"

She hesitated, taking her gloves out of her bag.

"I'm checking into the hospital tomorrow morning."

Silence.

"Can I visit you?"

"Are you sure you want to? You always hated hospitals. Don't you remember when I was admitted with appendicitis? Don't you remember how hard you found it to come and visit me?"

"That was a long time ago."

"Are you sure? I don't want your pity."

"I don't pity you. I just want to see you."

She smiled, then wrote the name and the address of the hospital on a piece of paper.

"You can always change your mind," she said. "I won't blame you if you do."

"I won't. I'll be there."

She put her arms around him again, hugging him like before and kissing him on the cheek.

"I'm so glad we met this evening," she said.

He watched her leave and remained standing for a long time without moving.

He lay awake in bed until the early hours when, no longer able to contain himself, he got up, packed his case, washed and paid for the room. It was still dark outside. The lobby was empty except for the receptionist and a porter. Before leaving, Tomas looked into the empty library. He pictured her in the chair, her pale cheek, the delicate veins in her neck. When he began to shake he pulled himself together, grabbed his briefcase and hurried to the taxi outside.

It was just after five. His flight to Chicago wasn't till nine. The weather was still cold but the forecast was good. At this time of year you never knew if that would hold.

february

They arrived on a Saturday. The weather was still and bright, and after they had taken their bags into the house they went down to the sea and walked on the beach. It was quiet there and they met no one but a man walking his dog; he was polite and bid them good afternoon and they both returned his greeting. They didn't have much to say to each other but both found the sea air refreshing. It occurred to Jon to offer her his hand when the man with the dog had gone but he decided against it and put it back in his pocket. They weren't in the habit of holding hands so it didn't seem right for him to suggest they do so now. He stopped once and skimmed a few stones, and she watched for a while before slowly walking on. It was cold and the sky was slowly darkening.

Their house stood by the edge of a wood, not far from a small village on the south fork of Long Island. It was less than ten minutes' drive from the beach but a good twenty by bike. They used to bike there with the children in summer, had done so since they were small.

The boy was now sixteen, the girl fourteen. In summer they could buy vegetables by the road to the beach, and in August corn and sun-flowers. There were fields on both sides and the soil was fertile. They didn't usually go to their country house in winter, and Jon commented on the way back from the beach how empty everything seemed. Crows circled over the gray fields, the stalls of the produce sellers stood bare at the side of the road and in the window of one of the stores on the way a hand-painted sign read: CLOSED TILL MAY 1ST.

"Still, it's always good to come here," said Jon.

They cooked together in the evening and after eating watched a movie on television. It had been cold in the house when they came back from the beach, but the heat soon came up and Jon got a fire going as well. Linda called the children; they were fine and had plenty to do. They had lived in Manhattan since they were born and had many friends in town. They no longer enjoyed going to the country on weekends. This time their parents hadn't suggested they come, let alone put pressure on them. Relieved, the children hadn't asked any questions. For all they knew everything was fine; their parents had tried to behave normally in front of them.

The counselor they had seen had encouraged them to go on vacation together. He talked sensibly, and Jon was quick to agree. He suggested they go to Florida. Linda hesitated. She didn't want to do anything rash, though she was just as concerned to save their marriage as he was. Jon reacted badly. He said Linda had no inten-tion of making peace, but the counselor intervened and pointed out to him that it had been only two weeks since the crisis.

"Maybe we could go to the country," said Linda. "There's a long weekend coming up."

The counselor had emphasized that they shouldn't even attempt to solve their problems all at once. It would take time, he said, and pushing things would be unwise. He encouraged them to speak their minds but not to feel any obligation to engage in serious conversation. "It's enough for you just to be together," he said.

He said much more in this vein, but Linda was having difficulty concentrating and most of it went over her head. She was thinking about the weekend ahead. She was already regretting her suggestion.

Jon and Linda had decided to tell no one but the counselor about their problems because word gets around. But Linda had made an exception and told her friend Mary, who lived on the floor below. Mary lived alone in a big apartment she had inherited from her parents, along with a lot of money. She didn't have to work, and although she had been married when she was younger she had no children. Mary had been very understanding and careful not to pretend to have any easy answers. Linda felt better after their talks.

"I'm not ready to spend the weekend alone with him," Linda said.

"What will he say if you change your mind?" Mary asked.

"He wanted to go to Florida."

"So who suggested the country?"

Linda hesitated before answering.

"I did. It was a mistake."

"The beach is always nice," Mary said. "Even in winter."

When the movie was over Linda went to bed. Jon spent a few minutes on the computer and by the time he went upstairs he could tell from her breathing that she was already asleep. He was always amazed at how quickly she dropped off and concluded that she must have trained herself to do that when she was younger and worked shifts. She was a doctor; he was an architect and painted landscapes in his free time. His paintings had been praised by knowledgeable people.

It was snowing when they woke up on Sunday morning. They drove into the village, bought the Sunday paper and bread and coffee and then went down to the harbor to look at the few boats still at their moorings. By the time they came home and sat down by the kitchen window to eat breakfast and read the paper, the lawn outside had turned white. Jon commented on how peaceful it was and how beautiful the yard looked in the snow. They looked out as they drank their coffee and Jon went to get more wood for the fire.

"We should come here more often in winter," he said.

She nodded absentmindedly and continued reading the paper.

"We don't use the house nearly enough," he added.

"What about the kids?" she asked.

"If they don't want to come they can just stay in town."

"They're at a sensitive age," she said. "Helen especially."

"Every age is sensitive."

They read in silence for a while.

"What play is it you're reading about?" he asked.

"I'm not, I'm reading about an exhibition," she replied.

"We used to go to the theater all the time," he said. "Why did we stop?"

"I don't know," she said, glancing out the window. "It's still snowing."

"Yes, really coming down," he said. "They didn't forecast this."

They both looked out, then carried on reading. The snow had begun to settle on the branches of the big fir trees in the yard, and the path to the house was no longer visible. Apart from the crackling of the fire there was silence, as if the snow had muffled all sound.

"The roads might close," she said.

"But we'll be fine," he said. "Do you remember when we got snowed in and Helen thought we would starve?"

"Yes," she said.

"We made a snowman with the kids," he said.

"An igloo," she said.

"And the car got stuck when we tried to drive back to town."

He smiled at the memory. She smiled too.

"Are you thinking of buying or selling?" she asked.

"What?"

"You don't usually read the real estate section from beginning to end."

"It doesn't make sense," he said. "Prices just keep going up. Not only in the city but in the suburbs as well."

"In Queens too?"

"Queens?"

"Do they keep going up there too?"

"Everywhere," he said. "The city and all the suburbs."

"She lives in Queens, doesn't she?"

He looked at her.

"Didn't you say it was there you went to meet her?"

He reached for his coffee without answering.

"How much have prices gone up in Queens?"

"Do you have to do this?"

"Aren't we trying to have a conversation? You ask me what I'm reading and I ask you what you're reading. Then we look at the snow."

"What does it matter if she lives in Queens?"

"It matters because I want to see where she lives. I want you to take me there."

He got up.

"I thought we were going to try," he said. "I thought that's why we came here."

"That was before it started snowing."

She stood up and went into the bathroom. He folded the real estate section and threw it on the fire. It blazed up in an instant. He sat down again and looked out at the yard.

When she came back she paused in the doorway.

"What is it that you want?" he asked.

"To go back to the city before we get snowed in, and to stop in Queens on the way."

"You can't be serious."

"Yes. I'm serious."

"And then what? What happens after that?"

"Then everything will be all right."

"After we've been to Queens?"

"Yes."

"Then everything will be fine and we can continue to try?"

"Yes."

"You promise?"

"I promise."

"Everyone makes mistakes, Linda."

"I know," she said.

He stood up.

"We'll have to wait till the fire's died down," he said. "We can't leave till then."

"I'll start packing," she said.

The firewood was dry and burned quickly. He turned down the heat, pulled the curtains and carried their bags out to the car once she had packed. He was wearing sturdy boots and warm clothes and didn't feel the cold.

The road to the house was nearly buried and he drove off slowly, taking care not to get stuck. Crows circled over the fields in the snow, black dots on a white screen.

"Not a moment too soon," she said.

"It's not like we'd have been trapped," he said. "I'd have called the Mexicans and asked them to plow the road."

It was heavy going at first but the traffic increased the farther west they drove. They had been driving for forty minutes before they saw the first snowplow.

"About time," he said.

She turned on the radio, moving from one station to the next, then turned it off again. Reception was always poor in this area.

"I think it would be best to go straight home," he said. "The weather's getting worse."

"No," she said.

"What if they haven't started plowing when we get there?"

"In Queens?"

"Yes, in Queens. What if the roads haven't been cleared?"

"Is there any danger of that?"

"You never know."

"You must know. In a whole year you must have gone there at least once when it was snowing."

He didn't answer. All he could do was keep the car on the road. If it continued snowing like this they wouldn't be home for another two or three hours. The fastest he had done it was in an hour and forty-five minutes, door to door. It was half an hour less to Queens.

The freeway had been cleared when they finally reached it, but the snow continued to fall heavily and the tracks of the snowplow had already begun to fill. They were running out of fuel so he stopped at the first gas station they saw and filled the tank himself. Jon asked the man in the truck next to him whether he knew what it was like closer to the city.

"It's a mess," said the man. "Even worse than here."

As they approached the city the radio reception improved and Linda found a station she liked. They were playing jazz, mostly fairly upbeat stuff. Between songs the announcer talked about the snow and confirmed what the truck driver had said.

"You hear what he says," said Jon. "It's worse in the city."

"Yes," she said. "I can hear."

"So you can imagine what it'll be like in Queens."

"No, I can't. I never go there."

He had been driving slowly but now unconsciously he sped up.

"Linda," he said, "it won't work if I have to be on my knees all the time."

She was silent.

"It won't work if you're going to use every chance to rub my nose in it. How many times have I said I'm sorry? How often have I told you that it was the biggest mistake of my life?"

"I just need to see where she lives."

"And then what?"

"Then nothing."

"Nothing?"

"Then we can stop talking about it and start going to the theater again. And to the country on weekends."

"Do you mean it?"

"Yes. I just need to see where she lives. Then it will be over."

He hadn't had much to look forward to in recent weeks, but her words and the tone of her voice raised his hopes. He stepped on the gas again and turned up the radio. Under normal circumstances he would have enjoyed this blizzard. He had always welcomed adventures, as long as they didn't involve any real danger.

When they approached the Queens exits she began to look around.

"Are we close?" she asked.

"Yes."

"You mainly came here in the afternoon, didn't you?"

They were still on the freeway and he moved all the way to the right.

"You see they haven't cleared the side streets," he said.

"What exit do you take?"

"It looks bad," he said. "I don't think it makes any sense to go there now."

"Hardly any less sense than your previous trips," she said.

He gave her a quick glance.

"Sorry," she said. "I shouldn't have said that."

He slowed down and got off the freeway. The snow fell heavily and the wind picked up. The cars parked by the sidewalk had vanished under the snow. Visibility was bad.

"This makes no sense," said Jon.

"How far is it now?" she asked.

"Not far."

Pause.

"Jon?"

"Yes?"

"Were you here when you missed Helen's graduation concert?"

He peered right and left, not answering immediately, as if he wasn't sure of the way.

"Can you please, please stop these questions?"

"I just want to know," she said.

"I can't remember. I can't account for every second of my life. I just can't."

A few of the main avenues had been cleared but the side streets were buried. They crawled forward, from one street to the next, past low-rise residential buildings, Chinese restaurants, a shoe-maker, a dry cleaner. Everything was shut, but the employees from one of the restaurants were clearing the snow from the sidewalk outside.

Jon was having difficulty seeing out the windshield and was afraid that sooner or later he would get stuck. He wiped the mist from the glass and stopped in the middle of the road. It was a one-way street.

"Well," he said.

"Here?"

"Yes," he said, pointing to a three-story house on the right.

She opened the window. The snowflakes blew in.

"Which floor?"

"Second."

"Which one? The one with the yellow curtains?"

He looked out.

"No, the white."

"White?"

"Yes."

She looked in silence at the iron fence in front of the house, the gate in the fence, the steps up to the front door, the white curtains on the second floor.

"Where did you park?"

"In the street."

"What do you think she's doing?"

"Can we go now?"

"We've only just arrived."

"We're in the middle of the road," he said. "You've seen where she lives now."

"Do you think she misses you?"

He looked in the rearview mirror and breathed a sigh of relief when he saw a Jeep coming up behind them.

"We've got to go," he said. "There's a car coming."

He drove off. At the end of the street he looked hesitantly in both directions before turning left. Linda looked over her shoulder. The road was icy. He turned left again and didn't realize until too late that he had come to a dead end.

"Damn," he said.

He couldn't turn around but managed with difficulty to reverse.

"Damn," he said again.

She looked at him. He stared through the windshield, turning up the wipers.

"Jon," she said, "what's the name of the street where she lives?"

"What?"

"What street were we on?"

They were approaching the freeway. Ahead he could see signs for the ramp.

She raised her voice.

"What's it called, Jon? Answer me."

"It doesn't matter."

"Turn around."

He drove on without answering.

"Stop! Turn around!"

She grabbed the wheel. He wrestled with her, slamming his foot on the brake. The car skidded, then stopped.

"Are you crazy?"

"Take me to her. Take me to where she lives."

He loosened his grip on the steering wheel. The windshield wipers worked frantically; on the radio the announcer was talking about the snow.

"I can't," he said quietly.

"Why not?"

When he didn't answer she repeated the question again and again until he thought he was going mad.

"She doesn't live in Queens," he said at last.

Silence. She stared at him. He looked away.

"She lives in the city," he said quietly. "On the floor below us."

Without a word she reached for her coat in the backseat and got out. He was going to go after her but didn't because he knew there was no point. As she vanished into the blizzard he sat without moving, listening to his last words echoing in his head.

march

The ski lift was next to the hotel. The sun was shining and they were sitting in the café watching the chairs streaming up the mountain. Most were occupied, but still there was hardly any wait at the bottom. The hotel had opened recently and in the brochure they had received when they made the reservations it was emphasized that the lift was exclusive to the hotel guests. The brochure also mentioned that there were other ski lifts at the top and a wide choice of runs: green, blue and black, something for everyone. There would hardly ever be any need to wait for a chairlift, and for lunch you could eat at a restaurant up on the mountain.

They had brought the brochure with them from Iceland, though they already knew it by heart and assumed it would be available at hotel reception. Jenny had leafed through it on the plane, and Karl had watched her read it and thought about white slopes and relaxing evenings. The brochure included more than one picture of guests gathered around a large open fire in the library. A stone chimneypiece rose to the roof; otherwise the walls were timbered. The guests in the pictures looked cheerful and rosy-cheeked after a day on the slopes, and the firelight enhanced their healthy glow. Most of them were wearing red or blue pullovers. A buffalo head hung over the fireplace.

Karl and Jenny had met on a skiing trip when they were twenty and had been skiing ever since. It was twenty-two years since they had married, but both felt as if it had been yesterday. It was a happy marriage; they had been through a bit of a rough patch when they were thirty, but that was now behind them. They had been planning a skiing holiday abroad for their twentieth wedding anniversary for ages, but when Karl had suggested saving for two more years so they could afford to go to Colorado and stay in a decent place, Jenny had agreed wholeheartedly. She worked for a bank and had come across the hotel's Web site after work one Friday. She'd had a picture of the hotel on her screensaver ever since. Karl was a manager at the electricity company. He wasn't as good with computers as his wife was, so he let her organize the trip. They planned to stay a week. There were two restaurants in the hotel, and she had booked dinner at the more elegant one for two evenings; the rest of the time they would eat at the less expensive one. She had also booked a massage for them both on Thursday.

The lifts opened at half past eight in the morning and closed at half past three. They arrived at the hotel in the early afternoon after a two-hour bus ride from the airport. By that hour it was too late to hit the slopes. They had dozed on the bus but all weariness had vanished the moment they entered the hotel. They were greeted warmly; a welcoming card from the manager awaited them in their room, with his handwritten signature under the printed message. A bowl of fruit sat by the window. Outside were the slopes, with the lift directly below. The receptionist had stressed that they had been upgraded.

After unpacking, they both stood at the window. Jenny tucked her hand into Karl's and they stayed there in silence, gazing at the sunshine on the mountain and the skiers descending the slopes. The next day they would have breakfast at seven and be out there by half past eight.

They were both disciplined—Jenny no less than Karl—and had decided before leaving home that once they arrived they would visit the gym they had read about in the brochure. But now that the time had come they could hardly be bothered, especially Karl. He lay back on the bed and asked Jenny with a smile if they shouldn't just exercise right here. She kissed him, saying they had the whole evening ahead of them. They put on their gym clothes and were downstairs by two.

Karl had been running on the treadmill for only a few minutes when he felt a sharp pain in his left calf, as if he had been whacked with a stick, and he turned around automatically to see who could have done it. A moment later he was on the floor in agony. People rushed to him and Jenny knelt by his side. Half an hour later the doctor came.

He was lucky. That's what the doctor said. It could have been a lot worse. "For a man your age," he said. "A lot worse. It's only the muscle. If it had been the tendon . . ." He shook his head.

"When will it be better?" asked Karl.

"It'll take some time to mend completely," said the doctor. "But you're lucky. At your age it's usually the tendon. Then we'd have to operate."

He got Karl a pair of crutches and told him to lie with a cold compress on his calf for the next two days and swap it for a hot compress after that. "For ten minutes every two hours," he said. "And don't put any strain on your leg. You can sit on the benches outside. There's a wonderful view of the slopes."

So now here they were, sitting in the café, watching the chair-lifts stream up the mountain. It was nearly half past three; these were the last few trips. Jenny had burst into tears when the doctor gave his diagnosis but now she was pulling herself together. The staff couldn't have been kinder; they had brought a stool for Karl's leg, and a bag of crushed ice. So now he was sitting with his foot up on the stool and the ice pack wrapped in a towel under his calf. They both looked up at the mountain. The sun was beginning to set, and the skiers descending the runs were chasing their own shadows. The lower slopes had thawed in the sunshine, but the forecast was for snow during the night.

"It may not be as bad as he thinks," said Jenny. "You may be better by tomorrow."

Karl gazed out the window.

"At least it wasn't the tendon," he said.

"No, thank God it's only the muscle. You may be better tomorrow. Tomorrow or the next day."

"Drink lots of fluid," the doctor had said. Karl finished his glass of water and Jenny immediately refilled it.

"I'll stay with you till you're ready," she said.

"Nonsense," he said. "Of course you'll go skiing tomorrow."

"No," she said. "I couldn't."

She seemed about to cry again and he tried to reassure her.

"There's plenty for me to do," he said. "I can go swimming and sit outside and meet you from time to time when you come down. I'm sure I'll be back on my feet day after tomorrow. It's only the muscle."

He hadn't seen her cry for years, not since they had had their problems. He didn't want to think about that, but every time she cried it all came back to him. He would do anything to prevent her tears.

They had tried to have children ever since they first started living together. A year after their marriage Jenny got pregnant but lost the baby. After that nothing worked until she started in vitro fertilization. It had succeeded and they had been over the moon, as one would expect. So it was a great shock when she had a miscarriage the second time. It was spring, everything was blooming, the migrant birds had arrived and were singing in the trees and building their nests. The doctor had tried to be encouraging when he told them it was almost out of the question that they would ever have children. He advised them to adopt. "I've seen what a good effect it has on people in your situation," he said. "You won't feel any difference between an adopted child and your own. You'll fall in love with it straightaway."

Karl had agreed but couldn't get Jenny to say yes. Each time he tried she wept and said she couldn't. "Why?" he asked.

"I don't know," she answered.

"She may get over it," the doctor said to Karl in private. "It often happens. Time heals the wound."

A year later, Karl heard about a sixteen-year-old girl in the countryside who was pregnant and intended to give the child up for adoption. A colleague of his at the electricity company knew her parents, who had been having trouble with her. Karl asked him to find out if the child had been promised to anyone. It turned out that it hadn't, and his colleague told him the girl's parents were prepared to meet him and Jenny. "I put in a good word for you," he said. "It's very important for them to see the boy in good hands."

"The boy?" asked Karl.

"Yes, apparently it's a boy," replied his colleague, adding: "She's got narrow hips. He'll probably have to be delivered by caesarean."

Though normally calm, Karl found himself suddenly full of impatient anticipation. His brother had twins, a boy and a girl, who had just celebrated their fifth birthday, and Karl spent a lot of time with them. The boy, whose name was Kjartan, was attached to Karl, who looked after him when he and his brother took the children to the municipal swimming pools in Reykjavík. He had taught his nephew to swim, and helped him dress. When Kjartan was four Karl and Jenny had given him a pair of skis. Karl had taken him skiing, first on a little hill close to his house, then to a mountain outside the city. The boy took to it easily.

On the day his colleague sent him a message from the girl's parents, Karl left work early and picked Jenny up from the bank. This was unusual and she asked him what the occasion was. He had meant to take things slowly and prepare the ground carefully but now he couldn't restrain himself and told her everything the moment she got into the car. She listened in silence and, taking this as a good sign, he said more than he had intended. He reminded her what the doctor had said about adoption, suggesting that they should go the next day and meet the girl and her parents, and he rattled on about taking a break from work to get their house ready and so on.

When he stopped talking Jenny began to cry. She turned away from him, burying her face in her hands. There were people in the parking lot, so Karl started the car and drove off. He pitied Jenny but at the same time felt she was being unfair. "Why not?" he asked. "Tell me. Why not?"

"I don't know," Jenny gasped between sobs. "I just don't know."

Karl had visited the churchyard the day before to tend to his father's grave, and now he blurted out before he knew what he was saying: "Then there'll be no one to tend to our graves after we're gone."

The next few days were difficult. Karl kept tabs on the girl's progress through his colleague. She gave birth to the boy in the middle of June. He weighed ten pounds, was twenty inches long and was delivered by caesarean. Karl almost went to visit mother and child but dropped the idea when he came to his senses. A couple from the local community adopted the boy. His colleague lost touch with his progress.

Jenny had always been fond of children but now that changed. She avoided them and, moreover, seemed hurt when Karl played with his nephew, Kjartan, as if she could read something in his face that upset her. She became miserable and kept out of the way. Gradually things improved, but Karl was always on his guard. He reduced the time he spent with his brother's family and disciplined himself to give no more time to the kids than necessary. He went skiing as often as he could and took up fly-fishing and golf. He did well at work. So did Jenny. They didn't talk about the past.

"We can eat lunch together out here tomorrow," he said, reaching for his glass of water.

"So you don't want to go home?" she asked.

"No. It'll be a good trip. Doesn't every cloud have a silver lining?"

They had supper sent up to their room and had an early night. Having taken some painkillers, Karl dropped off quickly and had a reasonable night's sleep. They woke at six. It was getting light; the sun pierced the curtains. Jenny drew them, revealing a cloudless blue sky.

She fetched some crushed ice, and Karl cooled his calf for twenty minutes before they went downstairs. The doctor had said ten minutes but, determined to get better quickly, he lay there longer, watching the morning news on television. The forecast was for sun during the day and snow at night all week.

He went outside with her and even knelt to fasten her boots. She worried that this couldn't be good for him, but he showed her that kneeling didn't put any strain on his calf. The glare from the snow was blindingly bright, and he put on his sunglasses as he watched her walk to the lift. She turned and waved to him. He waved back, then went inside and sat down at the table where they'd had breakfast. He still had half a cup of coffee left but it had gone cold. He drank it anyway, gazing out at the sunshine.

For the next hour the breakfast room was crowded. There was an atmosphere of anticipation, as always before a day of skiing. People pointed out the window at the sun and the white slopes and the lift waiting a stone's throw from the hotel. He timed it: the wait for a chair took no more than three minutes.

It seemed to be common practice for people to bring their nannies with them to the hotel so they wouldn't have to worry about their youngest children while they were skiing. Parents said good-bye to their children and nannies after breakfast and hurried out into the sunshine. The last to leave was the father of a young boy, a tall, thin man of around forty. He was playing ball with the boy and didn't seem to notice that he was holding things up until his wife had called him two or three times. She had her ski gear on and was standing in the doorway. Karl got up and left the restaurant at the same time as the man.

"Knee?" asked the man.

"No, calf," said Karl.

"When?"

"Yesterday."

"That's too bad."

"It's only the muscle," said Karl. "The muscle, not the tendon."

"I hope you get better," said the man.

Karl had discovered that it was easiest to walk sideways. This put the least strain on his calf. He didn't want to use the crutches; they merely confirmed that he was in bad shape. He hobbled out onto the terrace and sat down on a bench against the hotel wall. It was warm and he stayed there a good while. He saw Jenny come down a couple of times. She looked around for him the first time, but he decided to stay put so as not to bother her. The next time she did glance over at the hotel but went straight to the lift when she didn't spot him.

There was a ski shop by the back entrance. He had decided to buy new goggles when they got to the mountains. He hesitated for a second but then decided that this was as good a time as any. He felt somehow that it was more likely he would get back on his skis if he behaved as if nothing had happened.

It was quiet in the ski shop.

"What happened to you?" asked the woman behind the counter.

Karl automatically looked down at his leg before answering.

"On a treadmill?" she said and shook her head. "You won't really need any goggles on this trip. They'll be on sale a month from now."

He hadn't intended to spend much but bought the pair she recommended, without worrying about the price. They were top-of-the-line, suitable for sunshine, snow, sleet or rain.

"I've got a pair myself," she said.

He and Jenny had agreed to meet at noon and have a snack together on the benches outside. He took a seat in a good spot and watched the skiers while he waited. Everyone was ruddy-cheeked and tanned; some took off their ski boots on the terrace, which was dry and warm from the sun.

Jenny arrived at ten past twelve. She had met a woman on the chairlift and skied a few runs with her. The woman's name was Nancy and she was from California. Jenny introduced her to Karl.

"Jenny told me what happened," said Nancy. "You poor thing."

"It's only the muscle," said Karl.

Nancy left them, saying she was going to look for her husband.

"He wanted to do some black runs but I didn't dare," she said. "Not on the first day, anyway. We arrived yesterday, like you."

She left and he and Jenny sat down on the bench. Cooks from the hotel were grilling hot dogs, hamburgers and chicken breasts out on the terrace and Karl asked Jenny what she wanted.

"You must have worked up an appetite," he said.

"Maybe just hot chocolate and a sandwich," she replied.

"They don't have that sort of thing out here," he said, then, feeling his tone could be more conciliatory, added, "But we can order it inside and bring it out."

"Then I'll just have a burger," she said.

"I'll go inside and get a sandwich and hot chocolate for you," he said. "What kind of bread do you want?"

"I can just as easily have a burger."

He stood up.

"If you want a sandwich, you can have a sandwich," he said. "I'm not a cripple."

He bought a tuna sandwich for her and drank hot chocolate to keep her company. When they had finished Jenny applied sunblock to her face.

"Nancy said she burned when they were here last year," she commented. "The sun's so strong."

"Not inside," said Karl. "I'll be all right."

She looked at him as if she didn't know how to take this.

"Shouldn't I just stay with you today?" she suggested. "I don't need to ski any more."

"I've got plenty to keep me occupied," he said.

"And we can go swimming together when I'm done, can't we?"

He was lost in his thoughts and didn't answer. She repeated her question.

"Yes," he said finally. "Yes. Don't forget your gloves."

He went up to their room and put the ice pack on his calf, then headed down to the gym. He had meant to lift a few weights and perhaps stretch his calf a little, but when he got down to the gym he found himself inadvertently recalling the previous day. He went over to the treadmill and looked at it for a long moment. The accident would never have happened if Jenny had agreed to have sex with him. He would never have come down here, never have gone on that treadmill, never have injured himself. By now he would be on the mountain wearing his new goggles, with sunblock on his face.

He left the gym without touching the weights. On the way up to their room he dropped into the shop by reception where they sold various odds and ends and bought some painkillers. The woman who served him asked how he had injured himself. He said he had skied into a tree.

At three he went downstairs to wait for Jenny. He sat on the same bench as in the morning, ordered a beer and stared up at the mountain. The shadows were stretching down the slopes as they had the day before, and in the distance a jet trail was visible in the cloudless sky. The sun was still warm on his face.

Jenny said she could see a change in him when she came down.

"You look much better," she said. "You've caught the sun on your nose. Just from sitting here on the benches. You'll have to put on some sunscreen tomorrow. Nancy said she and her husband both burned last year."

She had skied with Nancy after lunch, and they had agreed it would be a great idea for Nancy and her husband to join them for dinner the following evening.

"She's so nice," said Jenny. "Shall I see if I can get a table for four instead of two?"

"Fine by me," said Karl.

"Her husband's an engineer. He seems really nice too."

Karl had another beer before they went swimming. Afterward he stretched his calf in the hot tub next to the pool. There was a bar there as well, and the waiter brought him a beer in a plastic cup to drink in the tub. Jenny joined him after her swim. As darkness fell it began to snow. They sat in the hot tub, watching the flakes floating down from the sky.

He put on a blue pullover before they went down to supper. They had booked a table at the cheaper restaurant and afterward planned to sit by the fire in the reading room. They ordered barbe-cued ribs and salad. Karl drank a beer with his but Jenny stuck to Diet Coke. He was beginning to feel a little tipsy and his mood had improved.

"Are you feeling any better?" asked Jenny.

Karl stood up and raised his leg onto the chair, stretching the calf.

"I couldn't have done that this morning," he said.

"Do be careful," she cautioned.

"It doesn't hurt," he said.

"Darling," she said, "I was so worried. Our holiday . . ."

"Our holiday is going to be fine," he said.

"You can't believe how happy I am."

After they had eaten they retired to the library. The seats by the fire were taken but they got places near the window. People were sitting around a bonfire outside, warming themselves. Karl and Jenny ordered coffee, and Karl asked for a brandy with his. He said he could hardly feel his calf.

"But you have to take it slow," said Jenny.

"I feel much better," he said. "Remember when I took the gold for slalom in 'eighty-four?"

When he had finished the brandy he suggested they go out and see the bonfire. It was still snowing, but people weren't letting this bother them since it was warm by the fire. Karl no longer edged along sideways but concentrated on walking straight. His strides were shorter than usual because it hurt when he tensed his calf, but there was no doubt he was walking straight. He drew Jenny's attention to the fact. She nodded and asked him to take care.

They warmed themselves by the bonfire for a while, then went up to their room. Karl flung himself on the bed and asked Jenny to join him. She said "in a minute" because she wanted to take out her lenses before going to bed.

"If you'd only come to bed with me when we arrived," he called from the bedroom.

She came out.

"What did you say?"

He was about to repeat his words but stopped himself.

"It's been on my mind," she said. "It's been constantly on my mind."

"Oh, come on," he said. "I was only joking."

"You've been thinking about it too," she said. "Otherwise you wouldn't have said that."

"It just came out."

By the time she came to bed he was asleep. He snored quietly and she examined his left calf before pulling the covers over him. She could see how swollen it was compared to the right one. "At least it's not bruised," she said to herself, though she didn't know whether that made any difference.

Karl felt awful when he woke up in the middle of the night. He had been sweating and his shirt was damp. He reached for the glass of water on his bedside table, then went into the bathroom and washed his face with a cold cloth. His calf was sore, so he walked sideways to favor it. His stomach ached too and his head was heavy. It was three in the morning. He climbed back into bed and lay awake for a long time.

When Jenny got up at half past six he stirred but didn't open his eyes. She moved about quietly and he dozed off again. It was stuffy in the room so she drew back the curtain from the corner window and opened it. Sunshine flooded in and a fresh breeze fluttered the curtains. She hesitated a moment, then sat down on the bed by Karl and whispered: "Do you want me to wait for you?"

He slept on and she stroked his forehead before heading downstairs. She met Nancy in the lobby and they had a big breakfast of omelets, bagels and fruit.

Although Jenny had brought her skiing gear down with her, she wondered after breakfast whether she should go up and see Karl, but decided to leave him be. "It'll do him good to sleep," she said to herself. She told Nancy that he meant to start the day gently, making no mention of the beer and brandy. "He's lucky it wasn't the tendon," said Nancy.

Karl got up at ten. His stomach and head were still rough. The hotel had stopped serving breakfast but he drank some coffee and a glass of water and sat down by the window. His calf felt worse than it had the night before. He knew he wouldn't be doing any skiing on this trip.

There was no one else in the coffee lounge but nannies and their young charges and the man he had met yesterday morning.

His son had a little ball that he rolled across the floor to his father, who rolled it back again. Karl watched them, then got up and stooped for the ball when it ended up under his table.

"Hi," said the man, "how are you today?"

Karl said there was no change.

"Our nanny has a stomach bug," said the man. "She's been throwing up all night. I've been so busy recently that I've hardly seen my son. I'm taking the opportunity to spend the day with him. We're thinking of going sledding."

"How old is he?" asked Karl.

"Three."

Karl had sometimes taken his nephew, Kjartan, sledding when he was that age.

"It's a good age for that," said Karl. "You can start him on skis next year."

"Do you have kids?" asked the man.

Afterward Karl wasn't sure whether he had hesitated before answering. He had a feeling he hadn't, though. He couldn't explain it.

"We have a boy."

"How old is he?"

"He's a teenager. Fifteen."

"Is he here with you?"

"No, he's at school. He couldn't come."

"I'm sure things change when they grow up," said the man. "Ray's our first child. We'd been trying a long time. What's your son's name?"

"Kjartan."

"How do you spell that?"

Karl spelled it out for him.

"Is that a common name in Iceland?"

Karl said it wasn't uncommon.

"My name's Conrad," said the man.

The boy rolled the ball to Karl. Karl rolled it back.

"Well," said Conrad. "We'd better get moving. We're going sledding on the slopes below the hotel. There's a little hill there."

"I might come and watch," said Karl.

"Please do, if you feel up to it," said Conrad.

The doctor had advised Karl to cool his calf for the first two days, then put a hot compress on it after that. Now that nearly forty-eight hours had passed since he had injured himself he wasn't sure whether to fetch a bag of ice or start the hot compresses. He did neither, took a painkiller instead before pulling on his walking boots and putting on his coat.

He met Conrad and his son on the slope below the hotel. They seemed happy to see him.

"Do you feel like trying?" asked Conrad.

Karl said he did. He slid down with the boy, then trudged slowly up the slope again.

"That was good," said Conrad. "I can see you're an expert."

Karl smiled. They took turns sliding down the hill with the boy. Karl's calf was feeling the strain but it didn't matter. He was happy.

At lunchtime he went to meet Jenny. Conrad was going to get his son something to eat and then put him down for a nap. He and Karl had arranged to meet at half past one. They had struck up a friendship while talking about skiing, sporting injuries (Conrad had undergone an operation after tearing his ligaments), Iceland ("Iceland's green and Greenland's white, right?"), but mostly about children and how to bring them up. Like many people who have kids late in life, Conrad was very anxious to do a good job and plied Karl with questions. Karl gave clear answers.

Jenny was looking for him when he came out onto the terrace.

"Where have you been?" she asked.

"I went for a walk," he said.

"You sound so much more cheerful," she said. "I was worried about you this morning. I thought you might have had too much to drink last night."

While they ate Karl looked at his watch from time to time because he didn't want to be late for his meeting with Conrad and his son. Jenny noticed and asked whether he was waiting for something. He said no. He was preoccupied, so much of what Jenny said went in one ear and out the other.

"Is everything all right?" she asked.

He said it was.

"You should get going," he added. "I'll see you later."

She seemed unsure but left at last. When she looked over her shoulder he waved to her before hurrying inside. He and Conrad had arranged to meet in the lobby. Karl limped there as fast as he could. Conrad and Ray were waiting for him.

"What do you say we go to the same place?" asked Conrad.

Karl agreed.

Conrad asked Karl about his son, Kjartan, and Karl didn't hesitate to talk about him. Conrad asked whether he was into sports. Karl said he was into basketball.

"Does he like any of the American teams?"

Karl said the New York Knicks were his favorite.

"Are you serious? I do a lot of work for the family who owns the team. They own Madison Square Garden and Radio City Music Hall too. I have a surprise for you before you leave."

The hotel was located near a small town, and they went for a stroll there once the boy had tired of sledding. In a small restaurant they ordered hot chocolate and muffins. Karl and Conrad had cognac with their hot chocolate. They talked some more about basketball, and Conrad repeated that he would have a surprise for Karl before he left. Karl asked Ray if he was interested in basketball. Ray nodded eagerly.

"He's been to two games with me," said Conrad. "We watched them lose against Philadelphia the other day."

"Do you want to come with us next time?" Ray asked Karl.

They laughed.

"Karl lives in Iceland," explained Conrad. "That's a long way from here."

It was after four when they got back. Karl hadn't noticed the time and now hurried out onto the terrace, where he had agreed to meet Jenny. She was nowhere to be seen so he went up to their room. When he didn't find her there either Karl concluded that she must have gone for a drink with her friend Nancy. Feeling tired, he lay down in bed. A few minutes later he was asleep.

He was still in bed but awoke when she came in. She asked where he had been. He said he had gone into town and hadn't got back till just after four.

"I couldn't see you," he said.

"I waited for you," she replied.

He was tired and closed his eyes again. He had been dreaming about Kjartan when he was small. In the dream he was his father. They were tobogganing on the slope outside the hotel, and Kjartan said he was cold. It had been a troubling dream.

"You're still coming swimming with me, aren't you?" she asked.

He said he was going to take a shower.

"How's your leg?" she asked.

He turned on the television without answering. It was the weather forecast. Sunshine during the day, snow at night. Perfect skiing weather.

"You remember we're eating with Nancy and Bill tonight," she said.

"Is that his name?"

"Yes," she said. "Maybe I'll forget the swim. Do you want a game of cards?"

"No, you just go swimming," he said.

"We have reservations at seven," she said.

She left. He lay in bed. The window was open and the cool breeze was refreshing. He saw the shadows at the top of the mountain. The sky was beginning to darken. When she had been away half an hour he got into the shower and stayed there a long time. Then he shaved and ran a comb through his wet hair.

"You look so much better," she said when she came upstairs. "Do you feel any better?"

"The same," he said.

"But you look much better," she said, indicating the bed with her eyes: "Shall we . . . ?"

"No," he said. "It's too late."

"Too late?"

"Yes," he said, after a short silence adding: "I'm dressed."

They were downstairs at seven o'clock. Nancy and Bill arrived a moment later. Nancy introduced Bill to Karl; Jenny and Bill had already met on the slopes. The waiter showed them to a table by the window. Karl limped. It had begun to snow.

"You've had a hell of an unlucky break," said Bill. "How are you?"

"Fine," said Karl. "Couldn't be better."

Bill laughed. Nancy and Jenny half smiled. It didn't escape Karl that Jenny had been discussing him with Nancy. He wondered what she had said.

"The conditions are fantastic," said Bill. "If you're better before we leave you must ski the back slopes with me. Nancy tells me you used to compete."

"I'd be happy to join you there tomorrow morning," said Karl.

They ordered an aperitif.

"I went on six different runs today and didn't have to wait at a single lift," said Bill. "Did either of you have to wait at all?"

The women said they hadn't had to wait anywhere, and Nancy told them about a man who had flirted with Jenny on the chairlift.

"Don't worry," she said to Karl. "He didn't get anywhere."

"I'm not worried," said Karl.

Jenny gave him a quick look. He finished his drink.

"It was hot too," said Bill. "I took off my jacket after lunch and was wearing only my shirt. Did you go out at all?"

"I went tobogganing," said Karl.

Bill laughed. "That's a good one," he said. "Tobogganing."

"I got a burn last year," said Nancy.

"You looked like a lobster," said Bill.

"You didn't look so good yourself, thank you very much," said Nancy.

They laughed. Karl and Bill each ordered another whisky.

As the waiter brought the starters, Karl caught sight of his friend Conrad across the room, sitting with his wife and another couple. He waved to Karl. Karl assumed their nanny must have recovered from her stomach bug, which meant he probably wouldn't have many chances to go sledding with Conrad and Ray again. Karl was surprised by how upset this made him.

"Who's that?" asked Jenny.

"A man I bumped into today," said Karl.

"What on earth made you go on the treadmill?" asked Bill. "I know I shouldn't say it, but what on earth made you do that with the slopes right outside and weather like we've been having?"

"Ask Jenny," said Karl.

"They arrived after lunch," said Nancy, and Karl got the impression she had nudged Bill under the table. "There was no point to start skiing by then."

"Cheers," said Bill. "Feel better."

"Cheers," they all repeated.

Bill was talkative. He told them about their children, a twenty-year-old girl who was at university and a teenage boy.

"He's arriving tomorrow," he said. "Perhaps he'll manage to ski with us after lunch."

"Do you and he often ski together?" asked Karl.

"As often as we can," said Bill. "He enjoys it and it gives me a chance to talk to him while we're sitting together on the lift. You know what it's like trying to connect with teenagers."

"No, I have no idea," said Karl.

"Just be glad," said Bill. "You're lucky to be spared that trial."

He laughed and Karl joined in while the women tried to smile. Realizing he had said too much, Bill quickly pointed out the window at the snow that was now falling heavily.

"The skiing shouldn't be bad tomorrow."

They ate their dinners, then ordered coffee and dessert.

"Great food," said Nancy.

"Fantastic," said Bill. "Thanks for letting us join you."

"That was Jenny," said Karl. "All I'm good for is creeping around, sitting down, getting up again, thinking. Mostly sitting and thinking."

"We'll be better tomorrow," said Jenny.

"We?" said Karl.

"You must ski with me before we leave," said Bill. "You can't mope around in here with everyone skiing but you."

When Karl looked around for the waiter he saw Conrad get up and glance in his direction before leaving the restaurant. His wife and the couple dining with them remained at their table. They looked over as well. The wife smiled. Karl nodded to them. It was obvious that they had been talking about him.

"Anyway," said Nancy.

"Yes," said Bill. "That was really great."

The waiter brought the check. Bill and Karl split it.

"You're lucky the dollar's so weak," said Bill.

"The krona isn't much better," said Karl.

They were just getting up when Conrad returned. He was carrying a bag and walked straight over to their table. He introduced himself.

"We had a good time with Karl today," he said. "Ray's still talking about what fun he had tobogganing. He was so tired that he fell sound asleep the moment he finished his dinner."

Opening the bag, he took out a hat, shirt and shorts. The clothes bore the New York Knicks' logo.

"I thought your son, Kjartan, might like this since he's such a fan. The gear was supposed to be for the son of our friends who are sitting over there with us, but I can easily send them another set when we get home. They live in Chicago."

He handed Karl the hat, shirt and shorts.

"They should fit," he said. "You said he took medium, didn't you?"

There was silence at the table. Bill seemed confused, but Nancy signaled to him to keep his mouth shut.

"Thank you," said Karl at last, so quietly it was barely audible.

He had taken care not to look at Jenny but now could no longer avoid it. He was still holding the gear, clutching it tighter than he intended. She knew what had happened, knew the moment Conrad mentioned Kjartan. When she looked Karl in the eye she was sure. Raising a shaky hand to her face, she got to her feet.

"Excuse me," she managed to say before her voice broke.

She walked hurriedly out of the restaurant. Karl sat still for a few moments, then got up too. Conrad was still standing in the same place. Bill and Nancy sat at the table, staring down at their empty coffee cups.

Karl hesitated a moment as if to say something, then abandoned the attempt and went after her.

Jenny had shut herself in the bathroom when he came upstairs. She stayed there for a long time, and when he put his ear to the door he could hear her crying.

He sat on the bed. She hadn't turned on the light when she came in, nor had he. He sat in darkness, staring at the strip of light under the bathroom door. He didn't look up when she finally opened the door.

"Why?" she said in a low voice.

"I don't know," he said.

"Has it happened before?"

He shook his head.

"Is it going to happen again?"

"I don't know," he said.

He realized he was still holding the sports gear but didn't put it down.

"Why?" she asked again, speaking to herself this time rather than to him.

He didn't answer, just continued to stare into space as if he were searching for the right words in the darkness. When he couldn't find them he closed his eyes.

The following day they went home.

april

They sat in the living room drinking coffee, looking out at the lake. Margret got up every now and then to check on their son. He had fallen asleep in her arms in the living room, and she had taken him into his bedroom and laid him down. He was sleeping peacefully, but she kept looking in on him every few minutes to listen to his breathing. When she couldn't hear it she put her ear to his nose and mouth. Only then could she relax.

They had started using the summer cabin just over a year ago. Margret's parents had a cabin farther up the hillside and had given them a piece of their land as a wedding present. Oskar had built the cabin himself. It had taken a long time since he was busy with so many other things. The cabin wasn't large but it was well situated, with an uninterrupted view of the lake. A hollow with a stream running through it and some tall trees, mostly fir and birch, separated them from Margret's parents. Although Oskar got on well with his in-laws he liked having the stream and hollow between them.

They had come down after work on Friday. The weather forecast had been uncertain, but Margret paid it no attention, knowing from experience that it could seldom be relied on. She had spent many hours by the lake as a child; her mother had stayed there in the summers with the children, and her father had come out as often as he could. She had hoped it would be the same for her and Oskar. Until this evening she had been confident that it would.

They were drinking their coffee. Oskar had his back to the window; the men who had rescued him and their son, Jonas, sat facing him across the coffee table. Margret was sitting beside Oskar. When she got up yet again to check on the boy, Oskar said: "Leave it. He's all right."

She gave him a sharp glance but said nothing. Once she had left the room Oskar said: "How about some scotch? A man can't live on coffee alone."

He was filling their glasses when she returned.

"Scotch?" he asked.

She shook her head.

He added a little water and ice cubes to their glasses. The water came from the spring below the hollow. It was delicious and cold, even on hot days, he told the rescuers while mixing their drinks. He also told them that he had built the cabin with his own hands, as well as installed the electricity and piped the water from the spring.

"The water at Margret's parents' place always had a muddy taste," he said. "But now they get their water from our spring."

Easter was behind them; it was the end of April. The earth was gray and the air raw, but one could sense that spring wasn't far away. It was light till around nine and then dusky for a while before it got dark. The snow was gone.

"Not a breath of wind now," said Oskar. "Cheers!"

Margret studied the men. One of them had bought the cabin next door to her parents' place earlier that year. They had seen him in the distance but had not spoken to him until now. Her parents complained that he had a noisy boat and roared around the lake while they were trying to appreciate the silence and sound of the Great Northern Divers.

"A banker," said her father. "Nouveau riche."

From time to time the new neighbor held parties with the barbecues pouring out smoke and people swilling beer and wine on the veranda—according to Margret's father, who spied on them with the binoculars that Oskar and Margret had given him for his sixtieth birthday. Margret had the same kind of binoculars. Her father reported that his neighbor had two barbecues, one coal, one gas. "He'll end up setting the whole place on fire," he predicted.

The rescuers had introduced themselves after the boy had fallen asleep. There hadn't been time before. The banker's name was Vilhelm, his friend, Bjorn. Margret had flung her arms around them while she was still frantic. Oskar stood to one side, watching.

"All right, all right," he had said. "No need to make such a big deal out of it."

The look she gave him did not escape them. The men exchanged glances and Vilhelm said: "Glad we could help."

They were both in their thirties and seemed to be in good shape. Vilhelm was fair, Bjorn a redhead. Their hair was short.

It had been after dinner when Oskar had suggested to the boy that they should go out on the lake. Jonas was their only child, just turned six. He was named after Margret's father and was thought to have his features. His grandparents had given him a fishing rod for Christmas, and Oskar had taken him down to the shore to cast a line in the lake. A couple of times they had fished from the boat. Jonas had caught his first fish last weekend, a small trout that Margret fried for lunch. He had been very proud of it.

Oskar had suggested the boat trip as they relaxed after dinner. They had eaten salad and lamb, drinking white wine with the salad and red with the meat. They were content. A sense of serenity had settled over Margret, who liked to nod off over a book when in the countryside.

"Wouldn't it be better to go tomorrow morning?" she asked. "It's already eight-thirty."

"We won't be long," answered Oskar. "I promised him."

She did the dishes, and Oskar finished his wine as he cleared the table. It had been a rule when Margret was growing up that people shouldn't go out on the lake when they had been drinking, but she decided not to bring that up now. She had mentioned it before, and Oskar hadn't hidden his opinion that her father's rules had no place in their home. Oskar was far from drunk, anyway, and Margret made sure that Jonas's life jacket was securely fastened before they went down to the shore.

She had been waiting for a moment to herself. She was in the middle of a crime novel and had strong suspicions about who the murderer was. As soon as they were gone, she took a seat by the window with the book and a bowl of raisins. By the time they reached the lake, she was already immersed.

There was a breeze and the boat rocked a little as they fished. They had no luck in the first spot and moved farther out. They got nothing there either. When the wind picked up Oskar told Jonas they should be getting home. Jonas begged to stay just a little longer. Oskar agreed, but the trout still weren't biting. "The fish have gone to bed," he said, "and so should we."

Jonas hung his head, disappointed.

"I never catch any fish with you," he said, "and you never do anything fun like the man in the white boat. You never spin around or anything."

The man in the white boat was Vilhelm the banker. He sometimes amused himself by making tight turns on the lake, and Jonas used to watch him, enthralled. "Bloody fool," said Margret's father, but this had no effect on Jonas, who saw the white boat sending big waves up the beach.

Oskar was hurt by Jonas's disappointment.

"Shall we do a few turns?" he asked.

"You never do," said Jonas. "You never do turns like the man in the white boat."

"Right," said Oskar. "Hold tight."

They weren't far from land when Oskar turned around, headed out into the lake and increased his speed. Keeping within what he thought a safe limit, he swerved to the left and right before slowing down again.

"Wasn't that fun?" he asked.

"No," said Jonas, "not like the man in the white boat. It was boring."

Oskar sped up again, heading for land this time. He was feeling irritable and wanted to go home. He opened the throttle as far as he could, then thrust the tiller hard right. The boat capsized.

They went under. Oskar gasped. He couldn't see Jonas anywhere when he surfaced. Then, hearing him on the other side of the boat, he splashed around to him. Jonas was coughing up water. Oskar gripped the gunwale with one hand and pulled Jonas to him with the other. The water was so cold that Oskar didn't see how he could swim to land. The boy was crying and kept choking on water every time a wave washed over them.

Margret didn't see the boat capsize. The murderer had struck again, this time with good reason. She felt more sympathy for him than for the victim. Eventually she stretched, put down the book and looked out.

She screamed, snatched up the binoculars and dashed out onto the veranda. First Oskar appeared, then Jonas. There was nothing she could do, but she set off down to the lakeside anyway. Trying to run despite the steepness of the slope, she quickly lost her footing.

When she got up again she noticed the white boat. She reached for the binoculars.

After nearly ten minutes in the water Oskar was losing strength. He had tried to hoist Jonas up on the side of the boat but couldn't manage it. Jonas was no longer whimpering, and Oskar was afraid he was losing consciousness. He was losing his grip on the boy. The water was glacial. One wouldn't last long in it.

Margret saw Oskar let go of him. Vilhelm had been careful not to get too close so the boat wouldn't bump against them. He and Bjorn were leaning over the side, holding out their hands. Oskar set off with Jonas, but being unable to hold on to him, he used the last of his strength to get to the rescuers himself. They quickly hauled him aboard, then peered around for Jonas. A wave washed over him and he vanished briefly, but then his head appeared again. Vilhelm jumped into the water, grabbed the boy and swam back. Then they returned to land, towing the capsized boat.

Margret watched the whole thing through the binoculars. She had been standing halfway down the slope but now sprinted to meet them. Without waiting for the boat to land she waded into the water and took Jonas in her arms. Speechless, she collapsed on the shore. As soon as the men got out of the boat she stood up and set off up the slope with the boy. Bjorn and Vilhelm followed her with Oskar between them. He was still weak and couldn't walk without help. When Margret reached the steepest pitch she stopped to gather her strength. Vilhelm let go of Oskar, went over to her and helped her up the last stretch.

There was a hot tub by the cabin, and Margret stripped off Jonas's wet clothes and held him in the hot water. Vilhelm and Bjorn borrowed some old swimming trunks from Oskar, and they all got into the tub with Jonas. They didn't say much. Oskar just stared out at the lake. From a distance the waves looked insignificant, and when the setting sun broke through the clouds they were struck with gold.

Vilhelm borrowed some dry clothes, jeans and a sweater, from Oskar. The jeans were too big, so Oskar fetched some rope from the toolshed. In an attempt to put a good face on things, he joked: "We'll make a country boy of you yet."

Oskar drained his glass. Bjorn and Vilhelm were taking their time, and Oskar decided not to have another until they had finished. He started talking about the fishing in the lake, keeping an eye on their glasses as he talked. As soon as Bjorn took his last mouthful, Oskar leapt to his feet and fetched the bottle and some ice.

"Another drop?" he asked.

Bjorn nodded but Vilhelm declined.

"We haven't eaten," he said. "The steak was on the barbecue when you capsized."

Margret, who had been silent until now, looked up.

"You didn't see it happen?" Vilhelm asked her.

"No," she said. "I didn't see."

Oskar tried to cut the conversation short.

"I bought this whisky in London last spring. We were there on a weekend trip. Glenlivet. Sixteen years old."

"It's good," said Bjorn.

"We had the steak on the grill," said Vilhelm. "I can't remember if we turned it off."

"Neither can I," said Bjorn.

"Filet mignon," continued Vilhelm. "A beautiful cut."

"We've got some leftovers from dinner," said Oskar. "Why don't we heat them up for you?"

"We ran out the moment you capsized," said Vilhelm. "The steak's probably burned to a cinder."

"I'll heat up the lamb," said Oskar.

"What happened?" asked Margret.

The men looked at one another.

"I didn't see," said Bjorn. "I was inside."

Margret stared at Oskar, waiting for an answer. She had hardly spoken to him since they had come in. He twisted the glass in his hands.

"I don't really know," he said. "I turned and must have been hit broadside by a wave. That sort of thing shouldn't happen. The boat's supposed to be stable."

He glanced at Vilhelm. Vilhelm was silent. Margret got up.

"I'll fetch the lamb," she said.

She checked on Jonas before putting the meat in the pan. She heated the gravy too and divided the rest of the salad on the plates, along with the lamb.

"Here you go," she said.

Oskar refilled his and Bjorn's glasses. Vilhelm was still nursing his first.

"People have died of hypothermia in a shorter time than you were in the water," Vilhelm said.

"I tried to hold Jonas out of the water," said Oskar. "That's probably what saved him. I was pretty cold myself by then."

He looked at Margret. She looked away.

"We must have been in the water for at least twenty minutes," he continued.

"It was less than ten," said Vilhelm. "We set off the moment you capsized. I'd been watching you."

"Really," said Oskar.

"I was watching you while the barbecue heated up."

"We watch you too sometimes when you're out in your boat," said Oskar. "My father-in-law thinks you set a bad example."

Vilhelm smiled.

"He's got a good set of binoculars, your father-in-law. He doesn't seem to have much else to do but look through them. Do you know what make they are?"

Oskar glanced around.

"Where are the binoculars?" he asked.

"Down by the lake," said Margret.

"Down by the lake? What are they doing there?"

"I was watching," she said. "I saw when . . ."

She broke off, got up and turned away from them. She was on the verge of tears but managed to bite her lip.

"It turned out all right," said Vilhelm. "Everybody's safe. Perhaps I will have another whisky."

Oskar filled his glass.

"How about a game of cards?"

"Yes, why not?" said Bjorn.

"I'm not playing," said Margret.

"Oh, come on," said Oskar.

"You can play," she said.

"We must be going anyway," said Vilhelm, handing Margret his empty plate. "Thank you, I was starving."

Their hands touched briefly and she said quietly: "All right, perhaps for a little while."

"Good," said Oskar. "Whist?"

"Sure," said Bjorn.

"Of course we could play bridge but that wouldn't be fair," said Oskar.

"Why not?" said Bjorn.

"I'm two-time Icelandic champion."

He began to shuffle.

"Then this should be a walk in the park for you," said Vilhelm.

Margret sat down diagonally opposite Vilhelm. Oskar shuffled showily, unaware of his wife's look of contempt. Vilhelm stood up and splashed some water in his glass.

"Are you sure you won't have any?" he asked Margret.

Oskar looked up. Margret noticed.

"Well," she said, "why not?"

"How about that," said Oskar.

"Ice?" asked Vilhelm.

She nodded.

Vilhelm handed her the glass and sat down. Oskar dealt, then suddenly looked up.

"What were you doing when we were on the lake?" he asked.

Margret didn't anwer.

"It was just luck that I happened to be watching you," said Vilhelm.

"She must have been reading," said Oskar. "Give her a book and she won't notice if the house is burning down."

He laughed. Margret looked away.

Bjorn and Oskar won the first couple of games. Vilhelm noticed that Margret forgot herself every now and then, her eyes straying to the window. Dusk had fallen but the lake was still visible.

"You've got better hands than us," said Oskar, "yet you still manage to lose."

Getting up, he fetched the whisky bottle and filled Bjorn's and Vilhelm's glasses. There wasn't much left but he took care to save a few drops for Margret. When he went to top off her glass she snatched it from the table and said quietly: "No."

"Right," he said, "in that case I'll finish it myself."

He and Bjorn kept winning. Oskar couldn't contain himself and pointed out Vilhelm's mistakes as he made them. He didn't usually behave like this, but he couldn't stop himself. Vilhelm listened with a half smile on his lips.

"Are you sure the engine didn't cut out?" he asked all of a sudden.

Oskar waited without answering.

"Just a thought," said Vilhelm.

"There's nothing wrong with the engine," said Oskar.

"What made you think that?" asked Margret.

"The boat slewed around so oddly," said Vilhelm. "I thought perhaps something had come loose. A screw, maybe."

Margret looked at them both in turn. Oskar stared at his cards. Vilhelm smiled.

"Let's finish this," said Oskar. "Who's out?"

"I'm out," said Bjorn. "Don't you have any more scotch?"

"No," said Oskar. "It's finished."

He saw that he was losing control of the evening.

"It's past midnight anyway," he added, hoping to get rid of them.

"There's whisky at my parents' place," said Margret. "You could go and get it."

"I don't want any more whisky," said Oskar.

"I do," said Margret.

"I'll go with you," said Bjorn. "I could do with some fresh air."

Oskar thought for a moment. He didn't see a way out.

"All right," he said. "Let's go."

Margret and Vilhelm stayed in their seats.

"We'll practice while you're gone," said Vilhelm. "We need it."

They walked quickly. Bjorn had trouble keeping up with Oskar. The temperature had dropped, and the wind was blowing off the lake, swaying the trees in the hollow.

"Where's the spring?" asked Bjorn.

"What?" said Oskar.

"The water supply you set up," said Bjorn.

"Over there," said Oskar, gesturing down the hollow without slowing his pace.

From time to time he looked back, though he could see nothing from this distance but a faint light in the living room window. There was a key to his in-laws' house hanging on a nail in their toolshed. Fetching it, he opened the door. His in-laws were in the Canaries. They usually went there after Christmas and stayed till May. The cabin held the usual smell of damp. Oskar headed straight for the cupboard where the drinks were kept and found half a bottle of Johnnie Walker.

He locked up in a hurry and returned the key.

"That should do," said Bjorn.

They walked back the same way. When they came to the stream, Bjorn remembered the binoculars.

"Shouldn't we go down to the lake and get them?" he asked. "It won't take us a minute."

They stepped over the stream and Oskar quickened his stride even more on the way down to the shore. After a short search they found the binoculars lying among the rushes where Margret had sat down with Jonas. They had just set off back to the cabin when Oskar stopped abruptly. Bjorn stopped too, and waited. Oskar hesitated, then raised the binoculars to his eyes.

There was no one in the living room. He searched outside the cabin too but found no one there either.

"Is everything all right?" asked Bjorn.

"Let's go," said Oskar, setting off at a run.

Reaching the cabin before Bjorn, he opened the door. He stopped short in the doorway, sweating and out of breath, when he saw Vilhelm and Margret in the living room, still in their seats. He was sure they had only just sat down. He thought he could see the change in them. Margret looked at him, then away again.

"You didn't take long," said Vilhelm.

"We ran," said Bjorn. "Oskar was in a hurry to get back."

"It's late," said Vilhelm, looking at his watch. "We really should be going. The whisky can wait till another time."

He stood up. The door was still open.

"Thanks for the lamb," said Vilhelm. "I'll return your clothes tomorrow."

When they had gone Margret remained in her seat, staring out at the lake. Oskar still hadn't moved. When he opened his mouth he had difficulty talking.

"What happened?" he said. "Tell me what happened."

She was trembling and didn't answer immediately. Then she buried her face in her hands.

"You let go of him," she said in a low voice. "That's what happened. You let go of him."

may

Before he knew it spring had arrived. The lawn in front of the house grew greener by the day, the trees bloomed and the wind was warm when they awoke in the mornings. There was a magnolia by the bedroom window, and he could see from its shadow on the curtains that the flowers had opened. He didn't mention this to his wife, Karen, because he didn't want to remind her of the arrangement they had made at the beginning of the year. They had hardly referred to it since, but of course he knew deep down—and thought he could tell by looking at her—that she hadn't forgotten. When he wasn't feeling well he sometimes imagined she was counting the days.

They had one daughter, Maria, named after his mother; Maria Jonsson, taking her surname from him, American-style, instead of the Icelandic patronymic. His own name was Johann Jonsson. Maria was at university in Chicago, but he and Karen talked to her on the phone every week and exchanged frequent e-mails. He had tried to teach her Icelandic when she was small, though of course she had forgotten it now apart from a few words—*blessadur* (hello), *takk* (thanks), *pabbi* (dad) and so forth. He didn't regret the time spent on those lessons, but recollected them with nostalgia. It seemed such a short time since his daughter had been a little girl on his knee.

Johann was an architect and Karen a psychologist. They had met at university and started living together shortly after they graduated. He had made an effort to maintain his relationship with Iceland while his parents were alive, but over the years things had changed. Daily life took over—work, child-rearing, marriage—and there were never enough hours in the day. He still attended Icelandic gatherings in their area though nowadays he went alone. Maria had lost interest when she hit her teens. He didn't blame either of them for their lack of interest and didn't push them to go. He himself used these occasions as a chance to keep up his Icelandic and talk to his countrymen.

He knew he was getting rusty. Although he couldn't hear the accent himself, he was aware that he had one and increasingly had to grope for the right words. The last few years he had started preparing for the get-togethers several days in advance, listening to the radio online when he came home in the evenings and reading aloud from books. Once he had recorded himself reading, but his voice sounded strange to his own ears so he didn't repeat the experiment. Nowadays he recognized few people at the gatherings but didn't want to give them up. Perhaps they reinforced his self-image, as Karen said, reminded him of his roots. He seldom felt galvanized by these meetings. Yet neither did they leave him feeling flat or regretful. They had less and less effect on him with the passing of the years.

When Maria was small the family had visited Iceland every couple of years but then stopped. Karen never complained about these trips, though of course it meant sacrificing other things; they had, for instance, waited ten years before going on her dream holiday to Burma. Johann had not been home since he had designed a shopping mall three years ago. The client was an avid salmon fisherman and, learning that Johann was from Iceland, suggested they go together. Johann had never been salmon fishing before, but since there seemed to be a certain glamour attached to the sport he greatly looked forward to the trip. They left on a Friday and returned the following Wednesday. It rained the whole time, the river was freezing, and although he caught five salmon he couldn't see much point in standing in a river with a pole in his hand from early in the morning till late at night. But he didn't complain. On his last evening in Iceland he dined with his brother and his family. They lived in a new house by the bay in a neighborhood that hadn't existed when Johann was growing up. The evening was pleasant, though he had been served pasta instead of the traditional roast lamb with peas and glazed potatoes he had hoped for. The brothers sat up late after the others had gone to bed, reminiscing about the old days. Johann was six years older than Thor. Although they had never been particularly close they had always gotten on well, and Johann felt Thor looked up to him. Before they said good-bye they discussed the possibility of Thor's coming to California before long.

It would be wrong to conclude from this that Johann felt like a stranger in Iceland or regretted settling in the States. He had always been content in California. He and Karen were well suited and had fortunately avoided any major disasters until now. Maria had been hit by a car and broken her arm when she was eight, but she had been quick to recover. And Karen had had some problems a few years back, but she got over it and took the opportunity to analyze herself and the effects of antidepressants during her illness. That was all, and Johann had told himself more than once that they were lucky.

They were early risers and began each day with anticipation and an open mind. When the weather permitted they sat outside in the garden they had been cultivating for years, drinking their morning coffee, reading the papers or just sitting and watching the day begin. There was a little fountain in the garden where the birds liked to splash, and it filled them with joy to watch their preening. Johann had assumed they would still be sitting there when they were old, sitting there in the garden each morning with their coffee cups and the papers and the birds in the fountain. That's how he pictured the evening of life, and he was far from dreading the future if they were fortunate enough to spend it together in good health.

So Karen's announcement at the beginning of January had taken him completely by surprise. No, that was putting it too mildly: it had been devastating. It was a Saturday. Maria had come home for Christmas and was due to leave the following morning. It was a fairly typical January day in northern California, cool and damp. It had been raining since Thursday, and Johann had gone into the garden that morning, standing in the shelter of the overhanging roof. The compost was rotting in the corner and the garden was gray in the rain, but he told himself it wouldn't be long before he could start preparing for spring. He didn't mind the winter, if you could call it winter in these parts; both garden and people needed it. Rather than make him gloomy the rain had a calming effect on him. He had been standing there for some time when he sensed he wasn't alone. He turned around. Karen was standing in the doorway. She looked as if she had been there for some time. She seemed pensive. He smiled at her, looked back at the garden then said he had been wondering whether they shouldn't add a flower bed beside the herb patch, a small bed, preferably featuring something red. She didn't answer immediately, and his thoughts remained on the garden until she cleared her throat and said: "We need to talk."

He turned at once because the tone was unlike her.

"Is everything okay?" he asked.

"Let's go inside," she said, "before we catch a chill."

It was quiet in the house. Maria was asleep. She had been out with her friends the night before and had gone to bed late. They sat down at the kitchen table, and Karen stared into her coffee cup, cradling it in both hands.

"We've always been honest with each other," she said.

He knew these words did not bode well but was quiet because he suddenly felt weak. When he stood up half an hour later he had to steady himself against the windowsill. The rain had stopped but he didn't notice.

Karen told him that she could no longer hide her feelings. She cared about him, cared about him more than anyone else, him and Maria. "You know that," she said. "That's why I haven't been able to face up to it till now."

"It" was her sexuality. She had been badly shaken when she had realized several years ago, or rather when she had admitted it to herself. Maria was then five, and Johann was talking about having a second child. She didn't give him an answer and, sensing her reluctance, he decided not to push her. He was happy with things the way they were.

She had been on the verge of telling him more than once but could never go through with it. Her parents had divorced when she was little, so she knew the disruption that followed. She told herself that she had nothing to complain about. Johann was a good partner and she adored Maria. Life wasn't perfect. She should be happy with what she had.

When Maria was a sophomore in high school Karen met a psychiatrist at a conference in New York. They had noticed each other at the opening reception and soon found themselves deep in conversation. Karen fell in love immediately. So did the psychiatrist. The pretense had been stripped away.

"You know who she is," she told Johann. "It's Janet."

Janet had come to visit nearly every year since, and Karen had visited her just as often in New York. Johann had never suspected anything, just assumed they were good friends and enjoyed her visits because Karen was always in such good spirits when she spent time with Janet. Now he understood why. He said nothing, unable to utter a word, just listened.

She took his hands when she had finished speaking. They were cold and damp.

"I'm finding this so hard," she said. "So terribly hard. It's as if someone's ripping me apart."

They wept together, leaning against each other, then Johann stood up, feeling faint. Karen remained sitting at the table. She had said nothing about her intentions or what effect this revelation would have on their marriage; that would come later. She just sat and tried to pull herself together after her tears, staring at the wet garden.

They agreed to tell Maria before she left. Actually it was Karen who suggested it, and although Johann thought it was premature he didn't have the presence of mind to do anything but nod. They waited till after midday. Johann went out before Maria woke up, aimlessly driving the empty streets, up the slopes above the valley and down again, stopping in a parking lot behind a shopping mall and sitting there for a long while without turning off the engine. When he came home they all sat in the living room. Karen told Maria everything. Johann stared with empty eyes while mother and daughter wept.

They had always been open with her and she with them. Before the day had turned to evening they were all feeling better. Maria was studying psychology, following in her mother's footsteps. At times Johann felt the women were completely detached, as if standing outside themselves. But then they slipped back into their own skins and hugged him, weeping. Maria asked whether they wanted her to delay her departure, but they both said there was no need. They went to a Chinese restaurant and tried to behave as if nothing had happened, at least nothing that broad-minded people couldn't cope with. They ate Peking duck and drank Tsingtao beer, and

Karen and Maria opened their fortune cookies while Johann paid the bill. On the way home it rained, and it continued to rain in the morning when Johann drove Maria to the airport. They talked about how it was their duty to support Karen and try to make the best of things. When Johann thought about their conversation afterward he felt he had taken no part in it.

Johann and Karen did not resume the discussion when he came home, nor over the following days. Perhaps Johann believed everything would go back to the way it had been before if they didn't reopen the wound. "Sometimes it's good to talk," he told himself, "and sometimes it's better to say nothing." Karen needed time to recover after her confession, so she was relieved when Johann made an effort to behave normally toward her. It was a busy time of year for them both, and hard work drives worries away. They lay pressed against each other as they fell asleep and were solicitous of each other's feelings. Maria called every evening for the first few days, but Johann asked her not to mention "it." She obeyed.

It had been two weeks since Karen's confession, and Johann had begun to hope the crisis had passed: she had needed to get it off her chest, he told himself, but now she realized that she would be happiest where she enjoyed security, support and love. Not caring but love. Having persuaded himself of this he was mindful not to behave in any way out of the ordinary, trying neither to ingratiate himself with her nor to make her feel remorse. One might have imagined this would be hard, suppressing a multitude of emotions, but he longed above all to behave as if nothing had happened.

But eventually Karen made up her mind. She said she didn't see how they could continue to live together. She couldn't do that to him. There were three of them in the house now, she said: the two of them and the deception. They would never be free of it. She said she also had to learn to accept who she was and try to forge a new life free of all ties. That's how she talked. She said she needed to find herself. That very cliché: find herself.

He glanced around while she was talking, at the floor and the sun streaming in through the windows. He had never dreamed that anything like this could happen within these walls; he felt as if he were somehow divorced from reality. Her words washed over him like so much meaningless buzz. He asked if she'd like some coffee. Coffee and the slice of cake he'd bought at the bakery. She was silent. He got up and went into the kitchen.

The next day she mentioned Janet. He asked if they were still involved. She nodded.

"I see," he said.

"Yes," she said. "I don't want to deceive you. We're having a relationship."

He was silent.

"I assume you don't want Janet to visit us." "Us," she said, not "me." He said she was right. She said she understood, though Janet was very keen to talk to him. He said he had no need to talk to Janet. He had nothing to say to her.

She brought up the house later. There was no hurry, she said; the main thing was that they should stand together and avoid conflict. She couldn't bear the idea that worldly goods should be the cause of bad feelings between them. He agreed, though he didn't regard their home as "worldly goods." But he didn't say this. He simply nodded.

That was when she suggested waiting till spring. They both needed time to adjust, she said, and she was sure they would find it easier to sort out their affairs when the sun was higher in the sky. Johann gave a sigh of relief, thinking she might still be vacillating. He said it was a sensible decision and they should use the time well. He didn't say for what and she didn't ask. "Use the time well," he said.

She visited Janet twice. He made no comment but felt sick to his stomach while she was away. They continued to share a bed but did not have sex. In fact their love life had become sporadic in recent years, but Johann had regarded this as a natural development;

they were both over fifty, and there was much else connecting them after all these years. Sex was only a small part of what they had together.

Now spring was here. It grew warmer by the day, and Karen started taking her allergy pills. In the mornings they sat outside with their coffee cups and the papers. Johann decided to dig the flower bed beside the herb patch. He told Karen, and when she agreed his heart was filled with hope. He bought both annuals and perennials, two small shrubs and new basil and coriander for the herb bed. He went out early one Saturday morning and by noon he had not only created a new bed, planted the flowers and shrubs and the herbs in the neighboring patch, but also mowed the lawn and raked the garden. He was feeling good after the physical exertion, the sun hot on his body, and fetched a glass of water from the fridge to sip on the veranda. Karen came out to join him and he was happy as they admired the garden together, until she said: "I really thought it would be easier in the spring."

She talked to the real estate agent the following Monday. He confirmed what they already knew, that there was a great demand for homes in the neighborhood. He looked at the house, which was in excellent condition since they were both extremely tidy, and predicted they would get a good price for it. He admired the garden. "We've been doing some work in it over the weekend," said Karen, then she corrected herself: "Johann has been doing some work in it." He asked whether they were moving far. They exchanged a glance. "No," said Karen, without elaborating.

Several weeks earlier she had suggested buying apartments close together because she couldn't bear the thought of not seeing him regularly. He had reacted well to the suggestion, but she hadn't mentioned it again. When the agent had gone she asked Johann if he had started looking. He said no, though actually he had looked at an apartment in a building that was still under construction not far from their home. There were two small flats for sale on the same floor, but he hadn't yet mentioned that to Karen. Perhaps it was just as well because she now announced: "I'm thinking of renting at first. I don't want to rush into anything." She said nothing more about their living near each other.

A young couple with two children bought the house. Johann made sure he wasn't home when they came to visit. They put in an offer the same day and weren't the only ones. The house went for a higher price than they had asked for, but Johann did not rejoice. He signed the contract the real estate agent put in front of him, studying his and Karen's names side by side before handing the documents back. The signatures looked odd to him. It was as if they had found their way onto the paper by pure chance and were now sliding apart again, especially Karen's name, which leaned away from his.

"It's certainly a good price," said Karen when the agent had left.

They were standing in the living room. It was still hot outside though it was after six o'clock. He wiped his brow and opened the window. "Yes, it certainly was a good price."

"What shall we do with the contents?"

He had assumed they would split their belongings, each taking what meant most; he hoped they wouldn't want all the same things. But he was silent, waiting to hear what she would say next.

"Why don't we auction them on eBay?" she suggested. "And hold a garage sale for the rest one Saturday? We could say good-bye to the neighbors at the same time."

He looked around. There was the corner table they had bought at an antiques store in San Francisco for their first apartment, there was the sofa where Maria always wanted to rest when she was sick, the bookshelves, the reading chair. . . .

"Unless you want any of this stuff?"

He didn't answer, unable to find the words, unable to collect his thoughts.

"Personally I think it would be best to start over," she continued. "For me, anyway. Leave it to our minds to choose the memories, not the furniture."

Afterward he wasn't sure why he had agreed to this arrangement. Perhaps he had been too stunned. Perhaps he hadn't wanted to appear sentimental when she didn't seem to care about anything they had owned together. He did say: "What about Maria? What does she want to do with her stuff?"

And Karen replied: "I've already asked her. All she wants to keep is her little armoire. She took what she wanted when she moved to Chicago. But she's thinking of coming home before we vacate the house. We'll sell her car then."

Maria's car was a fifteen-year-old Honda Civic that Johann had bought new and driven for years. Since it had never broken down or exhibited any quirks, it had seemed obvious that Maria should have it when she got her driver's license. It was blue but had faded in the California sun. Maria had painted a heart on one of the front doors and a peace sign on the other.

Karen had always been practical by nature but never more so than now. She began that evening to prepare the sale of their furnishings on the Internet and two days later had finished the task. She sat in front of the computer for hours on end, took photos, made inventories, wrote detailed descriptions. Johann watched her, moving from the sofa to the reading chair, from the reading chair to the dining room, saying good-bye to each of their belongings, remembering in parting each object's place in their life.

The auction on eBay took three days. Karen kept a constant eye on developments, filling Johann in on how things were going. So much had been bid for the sofa; so much for the dining room table; four buyers were bidding for the Italian corner lamp. He nodded but refrained from going on the computer until the last day. It was late in the day; he was the only one left at the office. He created a username and was on the point of bidding for the furniture when he came to his senses. Yet he stayed in front of the screen, watching kjones, vivip, sagestreet, vhill, uptowng and others buying his belongings. By seven o'clock it was all over.

Maria came home on a Friday. They were supposed to hand over the house after the weekend, and Karen had hung up notices around the neighborhood advertising the garage sale. Johann didn't like this American custom but said nothing. The house was in chaos so they ate out that evening. They sat in the restaurant garden, watching the sun disappear behind the hills above the valley. Karen talked about how fantastic Johann and Maria had been over the past few months. She also talked of Maria spending some "quality time" with Janet at some point in the coming weeks. On the way home they drove past the buildings where Karen and Johann had rented apartments. They were fifteen minutes apart.

When they came home Karen showed Johann and Maria how she had organized the garage sale. It was dark, but she turned on the light above the garage door so they could see. She was going to park the Honda in the driveway and line up the trestle tables she had rented on either side of it. She had measured out the whole thing; there was a six-foot gap between the tables and the car and enough room in front of it to put another, smaller table. She went into the garage and fetched a ribbon that she intended to tie around the car. The ribbon was white.

"Then we'll tie a bow at the top," she said. "You can keep what we get for it, darling."

Maria thanked her but it looked to Johann as if smiling were an effort.

"Well," said Maria. "It's late."

"Yes," said Johann. "We should probably go to bed."

They woke up unusually early the next morning to prepare for the sale. Karen seemed cheerful and Maria tried to pretend she was enjoying all the fuss too. But Johann could tell from looking at her as they ferried cutlery, vases, picture frames and old clothes outside that she was not happy. Nevertheless she made an attempt to smile and answer her mother sensibly when asked whether the candelabra would look best beside the china service or the rocking horse beside the bicycle Maria had owned as a teenager. She agreed distractedly, then asked if it was really necessary to sell the rocking horse. Karen looked up and said: "Take it if you like, darling. I thought you'd picked what you wanted."

"No," said Maria. "No, I really wouldn't know what to do with it."

Karen herself had taken nothing but clothes, books and three cardboard boxes of odds and ends. Johann didn't know exactly what they contained because he had been at work when she had packed them. They had divided up the old photographs, so perhaps those were in the boxes; it had been his suggestion, and she had asked him to sort it out. He asked if she would like to choose the pictures herself but she said she trusted him to do it. He did as she asked.

They were ready with everything by eight. Johann thought the ribbon around the car looked ridiculous but let it pass. He had parked the car between the tables, directed by Karen, who stood in front of him, pointing right or left. As he helped her tie the ribbon around the car he noticed that he had left the key in the ignition.

The people in their neighborhood were early risers, and the first customers arrived just as Karen, was ready to open shop, a group of women friends returning from a morning walk. He and Karen knew one of them and Johann went into the house when she started asking questions. When he came out they had gone, replaced by two young men on their way home from tennis; one of them bought some old inkwells that Karen had once collected, and the other bought a birdcage.

So passed the next hour. There was a dribble of people and things were selling reasonably well. Karen had said she was expecting most people between ten and one and now repeated this. Johann thought she was more hyper than usual; when the young men had left with the inkwells and birdcage she began to peer up and down the street in search of more customers.

"Things won't really liven up till ten," she said, more to herself than to Johann and Maria. "It'll be pretty quiet till then."

Maria had suddenly become immersed in some of her old children's books. "Perhaps she has forgotten about them," Johann said to himself.

Just before ten it began to rain. The forecast had been for showers in the afternoon but there had been no mention of any in the morning. Karen was prepared, nonetheless, having bought plastic to cover the tables and the items on the lawn. They fled indoors after hurriedly spreading it out. Maria said she was going to get some coffee. They watched her leave from the living room window, then remained there watching the rain after she had gone.

"I hope it won't last long," said Karen.

"Did you ever love me?" asked Johann. "Was it all a lie?"

"Johann, how can you talk that way? I still care about you. You know that."

"Didn't you ever enjoy sleeping with me?"

Silence.

"It was bound to come to this," she said. "You took it so calmly. You were bound to release your anger at some point."

"Don't talk as if you were at work," he said. "Didn't you ever enjoy it?"

"It's not about that," she said, adding: "Let's not talk about this now. You need a chance to express your anger, but we don't have time for it now. You have every right to be upset."

"I have a right to, do I? Thank you! And do you have a right to wreck this family after all these years? After all we've—"

"Not now," she interrupted. "Let's have this conversation tomorrow. We must do it right. The grief," she began, breaking off and starting again: "It's in our nature to get over setbacks. Even the loss of loved ones. We both went through this when our parents died.

We loved them and grieved for them but then they became part of our memories. That's how people are made. It's in our nature to get over the loss of loved ones. Otherwise we couldn't carry on."

"You aren't dead," he said. "It's not in a man's nature to get over it when his wife decides to become a lesbian."

Maria drove up to the house. Johann went into the bathroom and washed his face. When he came out the rain was ending.

"I bought you a coffee, Dad," said Maria. "Where's Mom?"

Karen was in the other bathroom. He heard the tap running inside.

"Is everything okay?" asked Maria.

"It's clearing up," he said. "Let's fold up the plastic."

The sun came out again. Karen emerged and welcomed the new customers. You couldn't tell from looking at her that anything had disturbed her. Johann found it unbelievable. That's what he said to himself: "Unbelievable."

"Nice to see you," said Karen. "May I offer you a cold drink? Yes, we're moving. Can't stay in the same place all your life. The lamp is eighty dollars, the vase forty."

Johann stood to one side, watching, then went back into the house and wandered through the empty rooms. Their bedroom smelled of disinfectant and echoed with his footsteps. He recalled that their marriage bed had gone for two hundred dollars on eBay. Maybe vivip had already started sleeping in it. He hadn't seen the buyer when the bed was fetched, and refrained from asking Karen what sort of person he or she had been.

There were more people when he came out again, and he saw that the customers were becoming competitive. He looked over the scene, his gaze not fixing on anything in particular until he spotted the picture frames. Several years ago it had been the fashion to fill one's home with photographs, but once this had gone out of vogue they had put the pictures in a box and stored them in the garage. Karen had been responsible for removing the photos from the

frames before the sale, but for some reason the two women standing at the table in front of the Honda, where the frames were laid
out, were evidently amused. He realized what was happening and
rushed over to them before he knew what he was doing.

Karen had failed to remove all the photos. The women were
holding their wedding picture. It was priced at five dollars. They
didn't notice him until he snatched the picture from them. Their
smiles grew rigid, and one of them was so startled she cried out.

People stared at him. He realized that he was screaming. He
had meant to unburden himself for months, but now his words were
tumbling over themselves. He had never heard himself scream
before. Gradually his voice cracked and the sounds faded away.
Maria buried her face in her hands, and Karen, who was coming out
of the house with a jug of lemonade, stood frozen for an instant,
then hurried over to him. When he saw her coming he tore the
white ribbon from the door of the Honda and jumped in.

He started the car immediately. People leaped aside in panic,
but Karen tried to reach him. Suddenly he saw her appear in front of
the car, as if she had emerged from a dark mist. He hesitated a split
second, then slammed his foot on the gas.

He felt the car hit something as he swerved out onto the street
but didn't know whether it was Karen or one of the tables. For the
first few seconds as he drove away he hoped it had been her. He
hoped it with all his might but knew instantly that after a few
moments this feeling would change. He would despair. He would
break down and ask himself what on earth he had done.

He didn't look in the mirror. The sun was high in the sky,
baking the streets. It didn't look as if there would be any more rain
that day.

june

Soley—Laura and Hermann Waage's youngest daughter—was married on a sunny day in June. The ceremony took place on the grounds of a popular hotel in the Hamptons, close to the Waage's country home. The breeze stood off the sea. The lawn stretched all the way down to the beach, green and closely trimmed by the hotel but rough where it sloped to meet the yellow sand. White chairs had been arranged in the garden with their backs to the ocean. There were many guests, more from the groom's side than the bride's, and most of them looked tanned and happy. The women wore light-colored dresses, the men light-colored suits, some with their shirts open at the neck and a handkerchief in their breast pocket in lieu of a tie. Behind flowering trees and expertly clipped shrubs, staff prepared for the reception while the minister spoke.

Soley was wearing the dress her mother and sisters had worn when they were married. Hermann had said more than once that this dress would be used only four times and his daughters got the message. His words were directed no less at their husbands, Charles and Michael, who were married to Ros and Disa respectively, and Lawrence, once he joined the family. The boys may have exchanged the odd joke about their father-in-law in private but they respected and even feared him a little, especially Charles and Michael. Lawrence didn't know much about him when he met Soley, but his brothers-in-law were quick to educate him. They were both lawyers like Hermann; Lawrence was a plastic surgeon.

Hermann was senior partner in a well-known firm specializing in corporate law. As a young man he had graduated summa cum laude from the law department at the University of Iceland and received a grant to continue his studies at Harvard. He had returned to Iceland after finishing his degree but stayed only two years, finding opportunities there limited. He and Laura moved to New York with one-year-old Ros and rented a small apartment on Madison Avenue between Seventy-eighth and Seventy-ninth. Later they bought a larger apartment in the same building, and later still a duplex on Park Avenue in a formidable building. By that time Hermann had made his name as a lawyer, becoming senior partner in the firm and adviser to well-known financiers. He avoided the limelight, giving rise to various rumors. It was agreed, however, that he was a relentless advocate for his clients and a formidable adversary. He was said to have a brilliant mind and a polished manner, and some thought his accent was Scottish. Though lean, he was tall and strong. He jogged regularly, lifted weights, had practiced fencing since he was at Harvard and was moreover fortunate enough to have kept a full head of hair. It was in the genes. He was graying a little at the temples, but that was all. He played tennis now and then but never went near a golf course. In his view golf was for retirees.

He adored his daughters, especially Soley, though she was supposed to have been a boy. He was suitably strict with them, adhering to a method of child-rearing that he termed "flexible firmness."

When they were little he had always made time to attend events that were important to them—parent-teacher conferences, school plays, ballet lessons, even doctor's appointments. At that time this was considered a mother's role, and some of Hermann's colleagues predicted that this eccentric behavior would cost him. But he didn't listen to them, relying instead on his own judgment.

His daughters loved and admired him, and felt sure that nothing bad could happen to them as long as they enjoyed his protection and care. He was a realist, so when they grew up he understood that there was no point in trying to block their romances. But it was their mother they confided in about their adventures, and when they were serious they asked her to prepare the ground for them before they raised the subject of their feelings with their father. Laura performed this service with the same adroitness she demonstrated in other areas. Hermann was always careful to speak to his girls in a businesslike manner. He found the most effective approach was to treat them like a client who needed help so as not to be taken advantage of in a business transaction. He had seen many a marriage fall apart due to overeagerness and inadequate preparation, as he told his daughters. They nodded. He wanted to meet their prospective husbands alone so they could get to know each other. Ros agreed without objection and so did Disa, after a little thought, and he achieved what he wanted from his discussions with Charles and Michael. He was pleasant but spoke his mind. It made it easier that they were both lawyers and understood his choice of words and appreciated his position. He talked to them like raw recruits at his practice, without pomposity but clearly in charge. Neither Charles nor Michael found this inappropriate; both simply were grateful that he did it in private and not in front of his daughters.

Laura had died three years before Soley's marriage. The end had come suddenly and she had suffered little. Hermann grieved in silence and tried to comfort his daughters, especially Soley since she was single and still lived in the city; the others had moved away with their husbands, Ros to Seattle and Disa to Boston. He took only a week's leave from the office and his performance was unaffected when he returned to work. But there was no hiding from those who knew him well that he was a broken man, and some commented that it was remarkable what a gaping vacuum a small, modest woman like Laura could leave behind.

She was buried in a small cemetery near the family's country home. She and Hermann had chosen the plot a few years before, after considerable thought. Hermann had always intended to be buried at home in Iceland, but when he mentioned this to Laura she pointed out that there would be no one to visit the graves; their offspring were all in America. Strange as it may seem, her words threw him because he had long convinced himself that they would go home in the end, though he had no clear idea when that would be. When it dawned on him that there was no going back, in this life or the next, he despaired for the first time in his life. Laura understood and did what she could to raise his spirits. Fortunately she succeeded and he soon regained his usual composure.

The same sense of despair flooded over him once more at the burial. Laura died in spring, when the frost had not yet left the ground. The trees were still gray and the paths muddy. They had chosen their plot in summer when the cemetery was full of life, and he recalled the hydrangea that had been growing in their spot. Now it was gone, and the cold grave gaped before him as the minister spoke. Ros leaned against Charles and Disa against Michael; Soley wiped away her tears at his side. He looked over the cemetery like a man who had lost his way, and briefly it occurred to him that his entire life was built on a misunderstanding.

Perhaps he had hoped that Soley would follow a path different from her sisters'. She was the only one who had spent her high school summers back in Iceland, living with Laura's brother and working in a shop and then a bank. She spoke Icelandic much better than Ros or Disa and was interested in what was happening in their homeland. Laura had told him Soley had good friends of both sexes in Reykjavík, and although some time had now passed, he was still fairly optimistic that she would find an Icelandic husband.

After Laura died he invited Soley to go with him to Iceland. She accepted and they landed in Keflavík one windless morning. He talked to her about how important it was not to forget one's roots and she listened, nodding. They stayed at Hotel Holt. It was there that she told him about Lawrence, over breakfast. Her sisters had had their mother for support but Soley was not so lucky. She had difficulty finding the right words and looked ashamed, as if confessing to a mistake. Hermann's initial reaction was understandable: silence, followed by a few short questions. But then he pulled himself together, got up, took her in his arms and held her tight. Although she was relieved, she knew she had disappointed him. That upset her.

Soley's initials were embroidered on the hem of the bridal gown beside those of her mother and sisters. Hermann caught sight of them while the minister was speaking. It was hot, and sailboats idled on the sea, waiting for a wind. As the bride and groom exchanged vows the waiters filled glasses with champagne. When the ceremony was over they walked among the guests with the glasses on silver trays. The groom's mother introduced Hermann to two divorcées who were friends of hers. He shook their hands, gallant as usual, but showed no interest in them. Those who knew him thought it highly unlikely he would ever remarry. He still talked to Laura when he was alone and hadn't yet moved her clothes from the closets in either the Park Avenue apartment or the East Hampton house. Her toiletries—half-full bottles of perfume, creams and cosmetics—were still in the bathrooms. Everything was just as she had left it, and his daughters had given up asking if he would like them to help him get rid of her belongings.

Hermann had not yet had a chance for a private chat with Lawrence. He felt an unreasonable resentment toward his new son-in-law and wanted to wait for this to pass. It was important for him to approach things with a cool head. He no longer had Laura to advise him and wanted to be well prepared. For Soley's sake it was important that they get off on the right foot.

During the wedding reception he decided to invite the newly-weds with him on a trip to Iceland later that summer. They had made other plans but didn't want to turn him down. He wanted to remind them both where Soley's roots lay, but he also thought the trip would provide a perfect opportunity for him and Lawrence to get to know each other better. Lawrence had been an excellent student and was already a successful doctor, but Hermann had the impression that although his son-in-law was polite to him he did not respect him or his world in the same way that Charles and Michael did. Feeling that this could have wider consequences for Soley and their marriage, he was keen to make corrections. Iceland could be the right place for that.

Soley and Lawrence went to France for their honeymoon. After a few days in Paris, they took a train to Provence. There they stayed at a hotel north of Carpentras overlooking a small country village surrounded by vineyards, and dined out on the veranda every evening. The moon rose huge and yellow above the mountains, and they gazed at it holding hands between courses and after the meal. Lawrence recited a Japanese poem about the moon and the stars, and alluded to Baudelaire as well. She was surprised at how well read he was.

When they got back to New York, Soley moved into his apartment while they looked for a new place. Lawrence had thrown away anything he thought might seem an eyesore—the plastic penguin he had bought on a trip with friends to New Orleans, a skeleton from his days as a resident at Lenox Hospital, an old red wine bottle with a candle in the neck. He had the apartment cleaned from top to bottom and got a female friend to buy various bits and pieces to make the apartment more welcoming. He also took care to make room for Soley's possessions and told her not to hesitate to chuck out anything she didn't like.

It was hot and humid in the city that summer. They enjoyed being alone and often ate dinner after work on the balcony outside their kitchen. Once dusk had fallen they lit candles and held hands. Afterward they made love in the half-dark apartment, and Lawrence whispered to Soley words that she was sure she would never forget.

They flew from New York to Iceland in mid-August. Hermann had arrived two days before. It was raining and autumn was already in the air. Lawrence was cold. He was wearing only a light jacket and hurried into a taxi when they emerged from the airport terminal after the overnight flight. It was Wednesday. They were due to stay till Friday. He was already looking forward to going home but didn't mention it, not wanting to disappoint his wife or his father-in-law. He had remarked to Soley that Hermann wasn't unlike his own father; he knew the type. He didn't elaborate, however, and she didn't ask.

This time Hermann booked rooms at Hotel Borg. He had planned to take Soley and Lawrence to the historic parliament site at Thingvellir and then perhaps up to the glaciers, or even north to Akureyri, where Laura's family came from. He changed his mind after reading a brochure in the lobby at the hotel about glacier tours and white-water rafting. He inquired about the tours, and the girl at reception said they were supposed to be excellent but that the white-water rafting wasn't recommended for people unless they were fit and healthy. She added that the glacial rivers of the Skagafjord area were the toughest and therefore the most popular with those who felt adventurous.

"There's a minimum age of eighteen on the eastern Jökulsá," she said, "and twelve on the western Jökulsá."

Hermann asked her to book a trip for three on the eastern Jökulsá.

Soley and Lawrence met him for breakfast as soon as they got to the hotel. It was still raining and the wind had started to gust. Lawrence looked out at the rain and asked what he felt were the required questions about the country and its people. Hermann's answers were detailed. He told his son-in-law about the Vikings who had discovered Iceland more than eleven hundred years ago, the literary heritage of the sagas, the "cod wars" with Britain over fishing rights, the hot springs, the powerful rivers and the longevity of the people, which he claimed was unsurpassed anywhere in the world.

"Is it the fish?" Lawrence suggested.

"Perhaps," Hermann said. "But maybe it's in the genes."

They looked out. A few cars crawled past; otherwise the streets were empty.

"It's very beautiful here in good weather," Soley assured Lawrence.

"It's always beautiful here," said Hermann. "As you'll see later today. Always beautiful, whatever the weather."

"We're going to Thingvellir," Soley explained to Lawrence. "Remember? The oldest parliament in the world."

"Actually, there's been a change of plan," said Hermann, handing them the river-rafting brochure.

They examined it. Lawrence got up and went to the bathroom.

"Dad, you know he gets vertigo."

Hermann said he didn't know but she needn't worry.

Neither of them was suitably dressed, so Hermann took them to a shop downtown that sold outdoor wear. He did the talking and paid for the clothes, despite Lawrence's protests.

"Has Soley taught you any Icelandic?" he asked.

"No," said Lawrence. "Not really."

"Don't worry," Hermann said. "We'll fix that."

They set off at ten. On the way north the guide, who was young and fit, outlined the day's program for them. It was his third summer on the river, and he said that foreign visitors were crazy about the rafting, especially Americans.

"Is it difficult?" asked Soley.

"Yes, but you won't have any problems. There'll be two of us with you. You'll enjoy it, I promise."

It rained nonstop until they reached the moors. Then the sun came out, and by the time they descended into Skagafjord there wasn't a cloud in the sky.

"Look," said Soley, pointing out the sea to Lawrence. "Look how beautiful it is."

"Unique," he said.

The drive north took over three hours. Lawrence dozed for the last hour. Hermann and the guide talked; Soley listened. The guide expressed an interest in taking up fencing. Hermann explained the basics of the sport and told him about a magazine and a Web site he could check out if he was serious.

"Do you lift weights regularly?" asked the guide.

"Yes, and I run," said Hermann. "You have to at my age."

"How old are you, if I might be so bold?" asked the guide.

Hermann invited him to guess. The guide considered, then underestimated Hermann's age by a decade.

"Thank you," said Hermann, smiling.

They pulled up to a hut not far from the river. The Jökulsá wasn't visible from there, but they could hear it. There was a rough pasture between them and the river, and the breeze stirred the long grass, sending waves across it.

There was another guide waiting for them. He was from Nepal and said he had taken the rubber dinghies down to the river. They kitted themselves out in wet suits, helmets and life jackets.

"Is this really necessary?" asked Lawrence.

The guides smiled.

"It's essential, you'll see," said the Icelandic guide.

"We've got some meat soup," he added. "Would you like some now?"

"No," said Hermann, "it would make more sense to wait till after we've had a go, don't you think?"

They walked down to the river. Soley slipped her hand into Lawrence's and said something the others couldn't hear. He nodded.

Once they had crossed the meadow the river appeared before them in a deep ravine. There was a steep path leading down to it. The guides indicated that they should hold on to the iron chains bolted to the rock. They went first, with Hermann close behind, but Soley hesitated with Lawrence at the top of the ravine. Hermann stopped and looked back when he was halfway down.

"Aren't you coming?" he called.

"I'll wait up here while you go," Lawrence told Soley. "This is not for me."

The guides had reached the bottom.

"Is everything okay?" called the Icelander.

"Yes," said Soley. "We're coming. Hold my hand," she said to Lawrence. "Try not to look down."

Lawrence did not take her hand but set off regardless. He inched his way, trying to look at nothing but the path at his feet. The sun shone in his face, and he shielded his eyes with his hand. Below him the river waited, smooth where the guides were standing but foaming white lower down where it plunged over rapids and small falls.

"Right," said Hermann once they were down. "What are we waiting for?"

They all managed to fit into one boat. The guides explained the rules and showed them what to do.

"Do we have to go far, Dad?" asked Soley in a low voice.

"Let's just see how it goes," he answered. "Lawrence will be fine. Don't worry."

Lawrence looked pale and held on tight to the boat as they pushed off. The river was smooth at first, but soon they hit some harmless rapids. Soley let out a cry as they descended them. It was a cry of pleasure. Hermann smiled at her and Lawrence, who was sitting in silence, clinging to the boat.

"See, there's nothing to it," Hermann called to him.

The sunshine was hot down in the ravine, but the water was cold. The river was in spate. As they glided along the guides pointed out landmarks. The Icelander asked Hermann if his son-in-law was all right. Hermann said he was fine.

After half an hour they saw some major rapids ahead. Lawrence leaned over to Hermann and asked if they could pull in to the bank for a rest. Hermann interpreted this as a cry for help and decided to be magnanimous.

"We'd like a bit of a rest," he called to the guides.

The river was still relatively smooth at this point, the banks flat and sandy. After they pulled the boat out of the water the guides brought out the thermos filled with meat soup.

"Thank you," Lawrence said to Hermann.

Hermann slapped him on the shoulder. Soley smiled at her father. Hermann smiled back.

They took off their helmets and drank some soup. Lawrence turned his back to the sun. Soley asked the guides about the rapids that awaited them.

"They're fun," they said.

"Dangerous?" asked Soley.

"No, not at all. We'll be careful."

"You just sit beside me," said Hermann to Lawrence.

"I suffer a bit from vertigo," said Lawrence. "The river's having an effect on me."

"You're doing great," said Hermann.

"I wouldn't mind waiting here while you carry on," said Lawrence.

"That's not a good idea," said Hermann. "Face up to your fears. Otherwise you'll never get over them."

Lawrence made no further protest. He sat in silence, staring at the river. Birds circled around the cliffs, their shadows gliding past noiselessly. Their calls could not be heard above the roaring of the water.

"Are you all right, darling?" Soley whispered to Lawrence.

He didn't answer.

Hermann made sure Lawrence sat beside him when they pushed off again. He passed him one of the paddles and showed him how to use it. The cliffs drew closer and the river narrowed. The current grew steadily stronger, tugging at the boat. They dipped their paddles in the water, but it was only for show, as the river was in control. The guides shouted words of encouragement, and Soley shrieked as she used to when she was a child. Or so it seemed to Hermann—she had always been the liveliest of his daughters.

Hermann saw what was going to happen when they were at the top of the rapids. He saw Lawrence lose his paddle and try to retrieve it. He saw his feeble movements. When he fell overboard he seemed completely limp, like a sack falling out of the boat.

Hermann threw himself in after his son-in-law. By then Lawrence was underwater, being carried down the rapids. Hermann went under too, but when he surfaced he spotted a red helmet submerged downstream. He made it there after a brief struggle with the water and dragged Lawrence ashore. The young man was deadweight and didn't move. For a moment Hermann feared the worst, but then Lawrence struggled to his knees and coughed. As he threw up some water Hermann made a show of thumping his back. Lawrence sat down on a rock and took off his helmet. It was dented from hitting a rock on the way down the rapids.

The guides and Soley couldn't pull the boat in to the bank until farther down the river. The way back up was tricky, but they did their best to hurry. Lawrence, meanwhile, continued to vomit water. Hermann asked him if there was anything he could do for him.

"No," said Lawrence. "You've done enough."

At first Hermann took this as an accusation, but once they were in the car driving back to Reykjavík he was no longer sure. He hadn't been able to tell from Lawrence's tone whether he was blaming him or thanking him for saving his life because Lawrence had still been retching when he uttered the words. Now his son-in-law sat silently staring out the car window. They were all silent. There was nothing to say. They were all aware of what had happened. The Icelandic guide had blurted it out. "He just panicked and froze," he said.

That evening they dined at a restaurant downtown. Hermann had called ahead and arranged for them to be greeted with champagne. He had begun to feel sorry for Lawrence and regretted not having just taken them to Thingvellir. He resolved to be as friendly as possible. It would be the prudent thing to do. He couldn't risk turning Soley against him.

He asked Lawrence about his job and showed an interest in what he had to say. Lawrence answered briefly, though politely. When they were eating their main course, Hermann said: "I hope your first experience of Soley's native land won't leave a lasting impression. I thought the trip up north would be fun. If I'd only known . . ."

Lawrence was ashamed but blamed Hermann for what had happened. He believed he knew all about men like him—men who always had to have the upper hand and found it impossible to relinquish control. He had more than once described his own father this way and accused him of being a bully. But that was a long time ago. He had only been a kid.

Although Soley was sore at Hermann and blamed herself for not intervening, she couldn't help looking at Lawrence differently from before. He had suddenly seemed so unlike himself, this strong and cheerful man. She was shocked. By far the most delicate of the three daughters, she knew she needed a steady hand. That's what her mother had said; before she died she had urged Soley to find a strong and determined companion.

Lawrence thought he sensed a change in her when they got back to the hotel. He thought he sensed it when they were in bed and he put his arms around her, stroking her neck, the hollow of her throat, her breasts. It had begun to rain again.

That fall Lawrence and Soley rented a small apartment in Manhattan, near Gramercy Park. It was attractive and bright, with a view of the park from the living room windows. Lawrence was working hard, and they rarely saw Hermann. Soley talked to him regularly on the phone, though, and also to her sisters. Although he always put a good face on things, his daughters, especially Soley and Ros, agreed that he was lonely. Disa, on the other hand, thought he was getting over Laura's death. He was attending con-certs more often now, she said, and was fencing almost every day. Soley had told them about the river-rafting trip.

"He panicked and froze," she said.

"Didn't you tell Dad he has vertigo?" asked Disa.

"Yes," said Soley, "but he couldn't have known that it would be a problem there."

"Dad's a tough nut," said Ros. "He thinks everyone else is like him."

"He saved his life," said Soley.

"I bet he enjoyed that," said Disa.

They laughed.

Hermann went on three dates that fall, all arranged by friends who thought it was time to introduce him to women they deemed eligible. One was the sister of a client. She was divorced, a few years younger than Hermann and considered glamorous. Hermann was bored by her at the restaurant they went to, despite the good food and the attentive service. He was bored by the other women too. He neither wanted to talk to them nor sleep with them. He missed Laura.

He met Marilyn by chance. It was at a hotel bar in the neighborhood, a first-class hotel with waiters in black uniforms. Hermann was returning from fencing practice and decided to have a drink before going home. It was something he did from time to time to postpone being alone in the apartment. He took a seat at a small table in the corner. She was sitting at the bar, wearing a short dress, and had her back to him. He kept an eye on her, waiting for her to turn around. She sensed that someone was watching her and held back a little before glancing over her shoulder. That was when Hermann saw how much she looked like Laura. Especially when she smiled and pushed the hair from her face. It was as if Laura had come back to life.

They struck up a conversation. She didn't chatter on like the women he had dated, but made do with a few well-chosen words. Hermann thought about her when he got home. He thought about her when he climbed into bed, and again the following day. Then he called and invited her to his apartment. She accepted.

The arrangement suited them both. Hermann wanted to please her and make her life easier, and she was not too proud to accept help. She was around forty and still very attractive, though she had been through the mill and had had her share of disappointments. She had no children and had been involved in the past year with a man who worked for the UN. He had disappeared to his homeland one day without so much as letting her know.

They agreed that she should come to him every Tuesday and Thursday evening at seven. He ordered dinner from a restaurant in the neighborhood, and they dined together without talking much. They didn't need to; they were at ease with each other, and the view from the dining room was absorbing enough. Hermann was always home by half past six on those days and changed his suit for slacks and a shirt that he could leave open at the neck. He slapped cologne on his cheeks and put a record on the turntable. He owned a CD player but preferred to play the old records he and Laura used to listen to. They were mostly jazz, Benny Goodman, Billie Holiday and that sort of thing. Marilyn was punctual in her own way, always arriving at ten past seven.

He was a considerate lover. It didn't surprise her. She enjoyed being with him and didn't have to fake her pleasure. Seeing photos of Laura in the apartment she couldn't help noting how alike they were. She understood the connection but didn't find anything odd in it.

After they had known each other several weeks Hermann asked her to try on one of Laura's dresses. It was a black dress he had bought for her in London when he was there for a conference. He had always liked this dress, so he took it out and asked Marilyn if she would mind trying it on. She did so willingly. The dress might have been made for her, and the same could be said of the other dresses, blouses and skirts that Laura had owned. It became a regular routine for Marilyn to dress up in Laura's clothes when she came to visit. First it was dresses and skirts, then underwear too, stockings, garter belts and shoes. Hermann chose the outfit when he got home from work and laid it out on the bed. When they had finished making love he hung the clothes back in the closet and she changed back into the clothes she had been wearing when she arrived.

It was a successful relationship. Hermann gradually opened up to Marilyn about Laura's character and habits, and Marilyn, being sensitive, tried to adopt them when she and Hermann were together. She had attended acting classes when she was younger and at one time had hoped to be able to make a career of acting. A lot of it came back to her when she and Hermann were together, and she welcomed the chance to playact with him, especially in the bedroom. It suited them both.

Hermann looked forward to these evenings and had to resist upping them to three a week, while Marilyn felt no need for affairs with other men. She worked in a jewelry store two days a week. The wages from this, along with Hermann's contributions, were quite enough for her. She joined a brand-new gym and ate out with her girlfriends regularly. For a long time she respected the arrangement with Hermann and didn't mention it to her friends or anyone else.

Their relationship could have lasted indefinitely. Occasionally Hermann asked himself if it was normal but was generally quick to ask himself in return what normal meant. He had seen it all and knew that the human soul contained many different compartments.

Marilyn wasn't sure why she started sharing things with Marta, the owner of the jewelry store. The two of them got on well but were not close. It happened gradually: first she admitted she had a male friend, later she revealed his name and finally she blurted out over a glass of wine after work that he was a widower and she sometimes wore his dead wife's clothes. When Marta demanded details Marilyn told her much more than was wise. Among other things she said that the man was Icelandic. She also revealed that he washed the underwear by hand in the bathroom basin after she had worn it during their sessions.

Some days later Marta remembered that the doctor who had made a few minor improvements to her face had once mentioned that his wife was Icelandic, but she thought no more about it until the next time she had an appointment with him. He was straightening her nose, but that didn't prevent them from chatting a little. She asked if she remembered correctly, and he said yes, his wife was Icelandic. Within a few sentences it became apparent that Hermann was his father-in-law.

Marta was loose-tongued by nature. The drugs and the local anesthetic didn't help, and her surprise at the coincidence made her even less discreet than usual. Before she knew what she was doing she had told Lawrence about Marilyn. Afterward she felt it was excusable in the circumstances but regretted mentioning the dresses, the underwear and the acting classes Marilyn had attended when she was younger. She knew she had gone too far.

Marta didn't mention this conversation to Marilyn. She half wanted to because it's always fun to be able to demonstrate what a small world it is, but she knew she had betrayed Marilyn's trust and thought it wise to keep her mouth shut.

Lawrence also said nothing at first. He wasn't vengeful by nature, but after the trip to Iceland he felt the need to restore the balance with Hermann and show Soley that her father was only human. Perhaps it was his imagination, but he had managed to convince himself that his relationship with his wife had been damaged by what had happened on the white-water expedition.

A few days later he visited the jewelry store. Marta had offered him a discount, so he bought a necklace as a birthday present for Soley. But he really wanted to see Marilyn. It was late on a Monday afternoon, and both Marta and Marilyn were in the store. Marilyn waited on him; Marta helped and shot him glances whenever Marilyn wasn't looking to confirm that this was the woman. Judging by the photos he'd seen, Lawrence found her resemblance to Laura uncanny.

That evening he invited Soley out to dinner, and although her birthday wasn't for another two weeks, he gave her the necklace he'd bought. It was warm, the streets were full of people and the restaurant opened onto the sidewalk. Soley was wearing a yellow dress and her blond hair was loose. Struck by how beautiful she was, Lawrence told her so twice. She smiled both times. A candle burned on the table between them.

He approached the matter carefully, smoothly turning the conversation to Hermann after he had given her the necklace. He stood up to fasten it around her neck and watched the candlelight gleaming on the chain. She had a beautiful neck and cleavage, and there was a shadow in the hollow at the base of her throat. It would be a long time before she needed cosmetic surgery. She kissed him on the cheek, and he returned to his seat. They raised their glasses. He told her about Marta.

She was surprised.

"How long did she say this has been going on?" she asked.

"Nearly a year. They meet regularly. In his apartment."

"He hasn't said a word about it. No one's seen them together. No one I know. No one Ros or Disa knows."

"I imagine they avoid being seen in public."

"Really?"

"Just a hunch," he said.

"You're hiding something. What is it?"

He filled their glasses with water from the carafe.

"Look, it's his own little secret," he said. "He should be allowed to live his life. You and your sisters don't need to know everything."

"What?" she said, her tone becoming insistent.

"She looks like your mother," he said. "Strikingly like her . . ."

Soley waited.

"Apparently she wears your mother's clothes. Quite literally," he added.

"What?"

"When she comes for a visit . . . apparently she dresses up in your mother's clothes and puts on an act. It's what your dad wants. It turns him on. Afterward apparently he washes the underwear himself in the bathroom basin."

Soley was silent for the rest of the meal. Lawrence left her alone with her thoughts. As they walked home in the warm dusk Lawrence talked about this and that, while Soley nodded, preoccupied.

Before they turned off the light that night Lawrence said: "Don't make a big deal out of this. We all have our needs. Even our parents. Aren't your sisters always talking about how lonely he is?"

It took Soley the whole night to work out how she felt about this news. Her sleep was uneasy. In the morning she called her sisters. As a rule she was easygoing, but now something had come apart inside her. Hermann and Laura's marriage had been a model for their daughters, especially for Ros and herself; when they had problems in their own marriages they thought of their parents' relationship as it appeared to them, of the quiet respect, love and solicitude. Soley couldn't help feeling that these memories had somehow been tainted.

Ros reacted as Soley did, but Disa made a show of being more sympathetic. She was a sociologist and less sheltered than her sisters. Moreover, she had confided in them that she had once slept with two guys at once when she was at college. All three sisters were drinking champagne when she told them, and Ros and Soley had squealed with laughter, though both insisted they would never dream of following her example.

"So what if he's having some fun?" said Disa to Soley. "Surely you didn't think Dad was sexless?"

"But this business with Mom," said Soley. "This business with the underwear. Mom didn't wear stockings and garter belts."

"Soley," said Disa, "how can you be so naive?"

Disa suggested they leave it alone, but after repeated phone calls the sisters agreed that Soley should talk to Hermann on their behalf. They had convinced one another that it would be wrong to hide the gossip from him. It would be embarrassing for him if word got around. He was understandably concerned about his reputation.

She called him at lunchtime on Thursday and asked whether she could come around that evening, she needed to talk to him. He asked if it could wait till tomorrow, as unfortunately he wasn't available that evening. She asked what he was doing. He didn't answer but asked in return if something was wrong. When she couldn't deny it he proposed they meet at once.

"Can you come to my office?" he asked. "At two. Does that work for you?"

She went to his office at two. There were handsome books on the shelves, paintings on the walls, a Persian rug on the floor and a vase of cut flowers on the coffee table, along with art books. They sat together on the sofa. He saw immediately that she was upset and asked what was the matter. She said she had heard he had a mistress.

"I don't have a mistress," he corrected. "But I do have a lady friend. Is that so bad?"

"No," she said, "that is not so bad.

"You know no one can replace your mother."

She said she knew that. He patted her shoulder. She hesitated a moment, then plucked up courage.

"Is it true she dresses up in Mom's clothes and tries to act like her?"

Hermann realized instantly that he would have to take defensive action. It was fortunate that she should have met him at his office, where he was accustomed to fighting battles. He asked what she meant. She explained, omitting, however, to refer directly to the bit about washing the underwear in the bathroom sink. He asked where this rumor had come from. She told him.

"Lawrence? He told you this?"

She made excuses for her husband, saying she'd had to force it out of him; the source was one of his patients whom Marilyn had told about their relationship.

Hermann stood up. Soley couldn't fail to see how displeased he was. He paused by the window and looked out.

"Soley, this is serious," he said at last.

She bit her lower lip, as she always did when she was nervous.

"You understand that I can't just take this."

She implored him not to do anything. She wanted to talk to Lawrence again; he had probably misunderstood the woman who had told him about it. She was probably making a mountain out of a mole-hill; the whole thing was probably based on a misunderstanding.

Soley called her husband the moment she stepped out into the street. He was removing a birthmark from a patient and couldn't come to the phone. When he called back an hour later Hermann had already made the necessary phone calls.

Marilyn promised to retract the whole thing and tell Marta she had made it all up, and make sure that if Marta spoke with Lawrence again she would tell him it was all lies. Marilyn was close to tears. Hermann was careful to let her hope that their relationship wasn't over, that he was capable of forgiveness. She couldn't afford to lose the income, and anyway she enjoyed the time she spent with him. He did not want to end the affair. He could hardly imagine a more comfortable woman to be with.

"What did you expect?" asked Lawrence when he finally got a chance to return Soley's call. "Of course he's denying everything. That's what I'd have done in his shoes."

"You'd have denied it? You wouldn't have told me the truth?"

"I wouldn't have told my daughter that I got a woman to act as my dead wife and then washed her underwear after I'd slept with her. Everyone needs his privacy, darling."

There was a silence on the phone, then Soley cleared her throat and told him she wanted him to call Marta back and she would listen in.

"I want to hear her voice," she said. "I want to hear her say this stuff with my own ears. Then I'll know if she's telling the truth."

"Why don't you leave it alone," Lawrence said. "This is none of our business."

But Soley insisted, so Lawrence called Marta when he got home. Soley listened in on one of the two phones in the apartment. Marta played her part well. She felt ashamed for having betrayed Marilyn and was determined to make up for her mistakes.

"Darling, you mustn't make such a big deal out of this," she said. "I wouldn't have mentioned it if you hadn't pumped me full of drugs. They made me all confused."

Lawrence was not fooled. He caught the false note in her voice and lost his head. He interrogated her, demanding to know who had made her change her story. He mentioned his father-in-law by name.

"What are you talking about?" she asked. He demanded that she confirm what she had told him about the acting classes, the dresses, the garter belts, the hand-washing in the bathroom basin. She said she couldn't remember saying anything of the sort.

"Why are you doing this?" she asked.

He kept trying to press her, but she was firm. In the end, she hung up on him.

In the spring, Soley and Lawrence separated. The decision was mutual. They couldn't put their fingers on what had gone wrong and treated each other considerately. Lawrence refrained from telling Hermann what he thought of him. He had recently met a woman who was a doctor like himself, and he was keen to start a new life with her as soon as possible.

It was sunny the day Soley and Lawrence moved out of the apartment in Gramercy Park. The breeze stood off the sea. They were still young and had not had time to accumulate what some refer to as worldly goods and others as junk. They divided up their modest belongings without rancor. The two of them stood alone in the living room after the apartment had been emptied. As Soley stared absentmindedly out the window Lawrence put on his jacket, then placed a hand on her shoulder.

"It doesn't matter to me anymore," he said, "but for your sake I want you to know that your father lied."

He kissed her on the cheek and walked out. She stood motionless for a long time afterward. The trees in the park were beginning to bloom, and the sky was red and pink as if in imitation. Lights came on in the surrounding buildings, and she saw people appear at the windows; from a distance they looked problem-free.

Hermann continued to meet Marilyn for a while but their relationship had been ruined. Their playacting had not been designed for an audience, and now they both felt as if they were being watched. Hermann suggested they take a break. He escorted her out of the building in the rain one Thursday evening and said goodbye to her on the sidewalk. They both knew they would never meet again. To Hermann it felt almost as if he were saying good-bye to Laura for the second time.

The bridal gown ended up in a closet on Park Avenue after Hermann had had Soley's initials removed from the hem. The dressmaker did a good job, and afterward there was no sign of the initials ever having been embroidered there.

july

Magnus Thor was a photographer, a tall, broad-shouldered man who seemed to dwarf the cameras in his hands. During his studies in France he had become fascinated by Lartigue, particularly his pictures from the Mediterranean. After graduating he headed south. He had just met Inga and invited her to go with him. They stayed at a small hotel at Cap d'Antibes, and Magnus used his Hasselblad to take pictures of her in the places where Lartigue had photographed his girlfriends in the twenties and thirties. The light was mild and warm, seeming to bathe everything in a translucent veil. When he developed the photos of Inga and saw her in that light he fell even more deeply in love.

In one picture she was sitting on the windowsill in their hotel room, wrapped in a thin sheet. It was a large window that opened outward. Outside it was a lazy afternoon; inside signs of the morning still lingered in the bed. Everything seemed so pure and innocent that the picture might have been taken before sin ever entered the world.

Back in Iceland Magnus held an exhibition of his photos. The cover of the exhibition catalog featured the picture of Inga on the windowsill, and on the back was a photo of himself. He had grown his hair in France and tamed it deftly. It reached down to his shoulders, thick but neat.

The exhibition was a success. It was reviewed in two newspapers, and the critics agreed that Magnus was a young man with promise. The picture of Inga was printed with the reviews. People who knew her were impressed.

It wasn't until afterward that rumors started about Magnus's similarity to Lartigue. Word never reached the papers, but it was not long before people in his profession had begun to whisper. Inga never heard the gossip but Magnus did. He felt under attack, but when he dug up his books of Lartigue's pictures he realized he had gone further in his homage than he should have. He was shocked, and for a while he came close to doubting his own talent. Inga sensed he wasn't himself and asked him what was bothering him. He said he missed France but didn't elaborate. She was practical by nature and shrewdly bolstered his confidence. Feeling better, he packed Lartigue's books away in boxes and put them in storage.

That autumn Magnus opened a studio in the center of Reykjavík. It was 1975 and things were quiet in the capital. Magnus gained a reputation for being artistic. His photos of bridal couples and children on the occasion of their confirmation, different but by no means revolutionary, drew attention in people's homes. He quickly became popular, and soon he and Inga were able to take out a mortgage and buy an apartment. The studio expanded and Inga found a job she liked. She was a nurse but avoided working nights.

The years passed. They had two children and moved into a nice house with a sizable garden. Magnus had plenty of work and was well known in town. He attended art events enthusiastically, with or without Inga, and pictures of him often found their way into newspapers and magazines. He still had a fine head of hair and had bought himself a trendy pair of glasses.

Memories of his photo exhibition vanished into the mists of time, and no one talked any longer about his plagiarizing Lartigue. With time decent people generally forget such mistakes, and Magnus was well liked by everyone he met. He managed not to let the memory bother him and concentrated instead on his work. He rarely took pictures for his own pleasure, let alone dreamed of holding another exhibition. Once fashion magazines had become established in Iceland he proved popular with their editors and was able to choose his assignments. He did numerous shoots for advertising agencies as well.

But as time passed he began to feel empty. The work had become routine. There was no challenge, but no threats either. The studio was doing well; he hired an assistant and had more than enough free time for himself. But it wasn't clear to him how he should use that time. He had long been interested in learning to fly-fish, had a rather glamorous view of the sport and decided this would be the opportunity. He equipped himself with waders, rod and flies, and went with a friend to the rivers Sogid and Laxa in Kjos. But he didn't take to fishing. The emptiness refused to leave him even as he stood on the bank, watching the river flow by. The persistent sense that something was slipping away made him grip the rod tighter than he meant to.

Inga, on the other hand, seemed happy. With time she cut back on work, started to attend lectures on history at the university in winter and applied herself to gardening in summer. She swam every day and went for long walks with her friends. The children had both left home; their daughter had moved to the west end of town with her husband, and their son had gone abroad to study in Britain.

Inga read or watched television in the evenings and was usually asleep by eleven. Magnus had difficulty focusing on TV these days and didn't read as much as he intended. One evening he went down to the basement and began to root around in some old junk. He wasn't looking for anything in particular but soon came across a box of photos dating from his years in France, along with photography books and catalogs. He was a little hesitant at first, but before he knew it he was absorbed in the pictures. When Inga called down to ask what he was doing, he said he was tidying up. He put everything back in the boxes, but the next day he carried them out to the car and took them to his studio. For the next few evenings he looked through them after his assistant had gone home. With his experienced eye he could see that some of the pictures came close to being exceptional, and this made him very thoughtful.

It was early summer; the evenings were light and the nights short. Inga had plenty to do. She worked at a health center in the mornings and spent the afternoons gardening or exercising. She asked him once or twice whether he was a bit under the weather, but otherwise left him in peace.

One day he finally decided to put his ability to the test. It had been a long time since he had taken a photo without being paid for it, and at first he was unsure. But he summoned up the courage, dusted off his Hasselblad and went searching for subjects. He took many pictures but when he compared them to the pictures in the boxes he was disappointed.

At the beginning of July he was asked to go to Paris on a shoot for an advertising agency. It was five years since he had visited France, and he felt in need of a boost, so he accepted the invitation gladly, though the fee wouldn't cover much beyond the fare and two days' living expenses. He was accompanied by a young model called Elisabet. She was around twenty, three years younger than his daughter. Magnus felt protective toward her. He had never been unfaithful to Inga, though he had been put in the way of temptation more than once. Elisabet aroused nothing but fatherly feelings in him. He knew men who had recaptured their youth, as they say, by taking up with women who were two or three decades younger than they were. He thought it peculiar but was too mature to judge them.

Elisabet was a vivacious girl who approached the world with open arms. She was interested in everything, big or small, and never tired of pointing out to Magnus things that caught her eye.

"Maggi, look!" she said again and again, tugging at his arm. "Look!"

They worked till late in the evening the first day, then ate together at a small restaurant close to the hotel. She was very impressed that Magnus spoke such good French and asked him to translate for her.

"How do you say 'I'm hungry'?" she asked.

"J'ai faim."

"And 'The chicken's good'?"

"Le poulet est bon," he said, adding: *"Vas te coucher tôt, comme ça tu ne seras pas fatiguée le matin."*

"What did you say?" she asked. "It sounded so beautiful."

"You should go to bed early so you won't be tired in the morning."

She laughed and told him she had arranged to meet a girlfriend who was working in the city over the summer. Her friend was going to show her the nightlife but she promised to be home early. "It's only eleven," she said. "I don't drink. You needn't worry."

She gave him a good-bye kiss on the cheek outside the hotel, then got into a taxi.

Their rooms were adjacent. Although Magnus was tired he couldn't fall asleep. After lying in the dark for a while, he switched on his bedside light and took out the book of Lartigue's photos that he had brought with him. Beside a picture from 1920 of a woman in a park were the photographer's musings:

I took one picture after another of Bibi in the garden, trying to convince myself that I could capture everything I wanted to and that

*nothing would be lost, neither the colors nor the beauty nor the per-
fume in the air. Nor the song of the birds. Nor the delicate flush on
her cheeks. Nor even my desire . . .*

Magnus had brought along a few photos he had taken of Inga
in the old days. He examined them in the light of the bedside lamp.
"My desire," he said to himself, "that's what's been missing."

He stayed awake until Elisabet came home at two. It had
started to rain, and he turned off the light and listened to the rain
on the window until he fell asleep.

At breakfast the next day he suggested to her that they head
south.

"It's on me," he said.

"Seriously?" she asked.

She called her parents and told them she'd be away two more
days. Magnus called Inga and said he'd be delayed.

"Are things going okay?" she asked.

"Yes," he said, "but it's raining today."

He omitted to mention that he and Elisabet were going south.

They took a flight the next morning, landing in Nice at midday.
Magnus rented a car and they drove straight to Cap d'Antibes,
where he had found an inexpensive apartment on the Internet. It
was by the sea, not far from the hotel where he and Inga had stayed
in the old days. They stowed their bags in the apartment and
changed their clothes. There was a sofabed in the living room, and
Magnus was adamant that he should sleep there and Elisabet in the
bedroom. On the plane he had accidentally let it slip that he had
waited up for her in Paris and she had teased him good-humoredly.
She did the same now and he smiled, then flung the big window
open wide and asked her to take off her clothes, wrap a sheet around
herself and sit on the windowsill. He took many pictures of her, and
although the light from outside didn't reach him where he stood,
his mind was filled with brightness and clarity.

Time passed quickly. He felt he was seeing everything with new eyes; his mind was open, and there was a spring in his step. He hardly put the camera down, though he was careful not to tire Elisabet out. Realizing how important this trip was to him she worked hard and encouraged him in her own gentle way. She had never been to the Mediterranean before and was enjoying every moment. Men gave her the eye and more than one tried to chat her up. Magnus was ready to come to her rescue but soon saw that she didn't need any help. He complimented her. She laughed.

"Thanks, old man," she said.

When they came home to Reykjavík he went straight to the studio to develop the shots. He should have started with the pictures from Paris because the advertising agency needed them, but he couldn't control himself. He had the feeling that the pictures from the Mediterranean would finally tell the truth about his talent, and he was very nervous. When he examined them in the darkroom his hands began to shake. He looked alternately at the pictures and his hands, so broad and thick in the red light. He was moved to tears.

He sent the Paris pictures to the advertising agency the next day. They had been skillfully shot but couldn't compare with the pictures from the Mediterranean. In his enthusiasm, he included two pictures of Elisabet from Cap d'Antibes in the envelope. In one she was sitting on the windowsill; the other was a side view of her standing on the beach, gazing out to sea. There was a boat on the water and a man in the boat, looking to shore. The sea was a mirror.

The advertisement appeared a few days later. In one newspaper it featured a picture from Paris, in another the windowsill picture from the apartment in Cap d'Antibes. Magnus read the papers over breakfast. Inga was getting ready for work. Since it was a sunny day she was talking about going straight out into the garden when she came home.

"Here's the ad I shot in Paris," Magnus said, and Inga came and glanced at it over his shoulder.

"Good picture," she said. "I'd better be off."

She didn't usually read the papers at home but occasionally got a chance to flick through them at the health center. She saw the photo of Elisabet at Cap d'Antibes just before lunch. She stared at it for a long time.

The moment she finished work she went straight down to Magnus's studio. It was just after one and Magnus had stepped out. His assistant greeted her with his mind on other things; he was busy serving an elderly couple who needed passport photos. Inga found the pictures from France on Magnus's work table. Feeling at a loss, she went into the bathroom to dry her tears. In addition to the pictures of Elisabet she had found one Elisabet had taken of Magnus in bed. It was early in the morning and Elisabet had gotten up before him and brought him coffee and a croissant. He was holding the coffee cup, bare-chested, with the sheet up to his waist and a smile on his face.

Inga waited till he came home. It was five o'clock. They rarely quarreled, and Magnus felt somehow detached, as if watching their row from a distance. It was predictable; Magnus defended himself but couldn't explain why he had not told his wife about his trip to the Mediterranean. He tried but didn't have the heart to tell her that all these years he had been ashamed of the pictures she had always been so proud of. In the end he wrote Elisabet's mobile number on a piece of paper and slapped it on the table in front of Inga.

"Call her," he said in a shaking voice. "Call her if you don't believe me. She could be my daughter."

He stormed out and didn't come home till late. By then Inga had spoken to Elisabet and was sorry about the whole thing. She couldn't understand why he had gone to their old haunts and taken pictures of a twenty-year-old girl in the place where he had photographed her when they were young, but she told herself that perhaps all would become clear later. Now, however, it was important to make peace.

"I called her," she said when he came home. "It was a misunderstanding."

He shook his head.

"What does it say that you trust a complete stranger more than me?" he replied, walking away.

Inga sensed something had broken. He sensed it too. He had felt his rage growing worse and worse as he drove around town thinking about his life—the terraced house, the garden, the photos of children on the occasion of their confirmation, the wedding photos, all that wasted time. He who never lost his temper now couldn't control his rage.

For the next few days he was rarely home. He answered curtly when Inga tried to speak to him, and she gradually retreated into herself, waiting for it to blow over. She was anxious, not knowing what to make of him. This made it hard for her to sleep. He came to bed later than usual, and they lay awake side by side with their eyes closed, listening to each other breathe. Once she tried to slip her hand into his but he pulled away.

After a week she decided to break the silence. She felt things were going from bad to worse and was afraid.

"Maggi," she said, "can't we talk about this?"

"What?"

"Can't we talk to each other?"

"It's too late," he answered.

"I made a mistake," she said. "I've apologized a hundred times."

"It's not that," he said.

"What is it then?"

"It's everything," he said. "Everything."

She was none the wiser but sensed that she was losing him. And she wasn't far wrong: he had begun to talk to himself about starting a new life, though he was still vague about what that meant. He was in too much of a state to think clearly, but it occurred to him to move abroad. He still hadn't thrown away the newspapers he had bought at Nice airport the day he and Elisabet had flown home, and now he read the property ads in them. There were apartments for sale at reasonable prices both in Saint-Paul-de-Vence and also down by the shore. He didn't need much. One room and a kitchen. And the spark he had rediscovered with Elisabet and was so afraid of losing again.

He had arranged to be sent details of several apartments before he fell ill. The real estate agent he talked to on the phone had been helpful and told him it would probably be best to wait till September before buying because prices fell once the tourist season was over. "But it's worth starting the groundwork now," he said. "Good apartments go quickly."

Magnus, who had always been a hypochondriac, tried to ignore the symptoms at first. The pains began during the night when he went to relieve himself, but he couldn't be sure whether there was any blood in his urine since he hadn't turned on the bathroom light. The next day, however, there was definitely blood, but he didn't tell Inga until two days later. It was the first time in two weeks that he had addressed her of his own accord. His tone had changed. Sensing his fear she was relieved, then ashamed of herself.

She called a doctor at the health center, who advised Magnus to come in for a checkup immediately.

"What can it be?" Magnus asked her.

"Let's hope it's nothing," she replied.

She drove him to the health center. He hated hospitals and had seldom visited Inga at work, preferring to wait outside in the car on the rare occasions he went to pick her up. On the way there his thoughts went to an old friend who had died from prostate cancer.

The doctor asked him some questions while examining him. When he was done he said he would have to send him to a specialist.

"What might it be?" Magnus asked.

The doctor avoided answering.

"I'll try to get you an appointment as soon as possible," he said and went out to use the phone.

Magnus was so weak with fear that Inga had to help him get dressed. She took his hand and helped him to stand.

"Don't worry," she said. "He'll do anything he can to get you an appointment right away."

As she wiped the cold sweat from his forehead she felt she had got him back.

She went out into the garden when they got home; he went to bed. Sunshine poured through the bedroom window, and the air was so clear that you'd have thought the good-weather clouds that passed by from time to time had been painted on the sky. She had opened the window before going out, and the breeze that came in was warm and mild, bringing with it the sound of children's laughter. It was the most glorious July day. He had never expected to die in summer.

He got an appointment with a specialist two days later. He kept going into the bathroom to check whether there was blood in his urine, and when the pains came he took to his bed. Inga tried to comfort him.

"If I get better . . ." he began once, but didn't continue.

"Of course you'll get better," she said.

"You know what it could be," he said. "It starts like this."

"I'm sure it's nothing serious."

"It starts just like this."

The specialist examined him and asked the same questions as the doctor at the health center. Inga had come in with him because he didn't want to be alone.

"Any bleeding?" asked the specialist.

"Yes."

"How often?"

Magnus told him. The specialist asked him to describe the pains and then said he'd have to do some tests.

Magnus asked the specialist what he thought it was. The specialist said he couldn't say, but advised him not to worry. "Let's see what comes out of the tests," he said. Magnus had the impression the doctor was avoiding his eye and felt his legs weaken.

A nurse came in and took a blood sample. Afterward Magnus went into the bathroom with a jar for a urine sample. He asked Inga to come with him. As they handed over the sample Inga asked when they could expect the results. The specialist promised to prioritize the tests.

"Right after the weekend," he said.

The next day Inga looked in Magnus's briefcase for some bills he hadn't had time to pay and discovered the French newspapers with the property ads. He had marked the apartments he was most interested in and scribbled in the margin the name and phone number of the real estate agent he had spoken to.

She stared at the papers for a while. She hadn't dreamed that he had gone that far. As she weeded the garden she wondered what to do. It was still sunny. When she looked over her shoulder she saw his face in the bedroom window. She waved to him. He raised an arm and waved back.

They ate supper at seven. He had little appetite. She said she had come across some newspapers in his briefcase, and asked what she should do with them.

"Throw them away," he said.

"Are you sure? Don't you want to read them?"

"No," he said.

"I'll put them in the pile I'm taking to the recycling tomorrow."

He was on edge all weekend. Inga's summer holiday had begun, and their daughter came to see them on Saturday. Magnus asked Inga to tell her he had a cold because he didn't want the children to know what was going on. He stayed in bed during her visit. Inga said he was asleep.

Sunday morning Magnus woke up before Inga. He watched her sleep and concluded that it wouldn't be right if he didn't photograph her before he died. She should be his last subject. She was still beautiful, and although the years had been kind to her they had sharpened her features. The pain having momentarily subsided, he felt a great desire to photograph this face in which he could now so clearly see their years together. He was convinced that he didn't have much time; the pain could return at any moment.

She woke up while he was watching her and smiled. After breakfast they went out to the garden. The light was pretty and the shadows too, and the birds sang. He photographed her for an hour without taking a break. Then he went to his studio.

He came back when he had developed the pictures. It was midafternoon, and he was very tired. He had read that the presence of death sharpened the senses and opened one's eyes to new dimensions, and he witnessed this now that he looked at the pictures of Inga. He was overwhelmed with emotion when he handed them to her and hurried to bed.

He waited for the phone to ring all day on Monday. At five Inga told him it was unlikely the specialist would call any later that day. Magnus was convinced this was a bad sign, imagining that the tests must have shown what he feared and that the specialist had wanted to repeat them in order to be sure before calling.

By midday on Tuesday he was in such a state that he couldn't cope anymore. The pain wasn't bad, and there didn't seem to have been any bleeding for the last couple of days, but this did nothing to lessen his misery. He thought of calling the doctor himself but couldn't summon the courage. Inga said he must try to think about something else, and asked him to go out to the garage for her and find some gardening tools she needed.

"It'll do you good," she said, adding: "They think it's going to be record temperature today."

She watched him walk across the parking area to the garage, diagonally opposite the house. She thought how fond she was of him. Yet she also wondered what would happen if the change in him failed to last. He could always buy more French newspapers. He could always call the real estate agent again. You never knew.

She looked again at the pictures he had taken of her in the garden. She liked them but wished she had had time to fix her hair. She knew they meant a lot to him. She was grateful for that.

Magnus had been gone only five minutes when the specialist called. He asked for Magnus first but when she said he wasn't home the doctor delivered the results of the tests to her. He sounded cheerful since the news was good.

"Does he have a family history of kidney stones?" he asked.

She said that her father-in-law had had problems with them.

"They run in families," said the specialist. "He was passing a stone, a bit of grit. It's not dangerous but it's painful and sometimes causes bleeding."

Before saying good-bye, the specialist suggested that Magnus come in for an X-ray to make sure there weren't any more stones in his kidneys or passing through his system.

"After the summer break," he said. "There's no hurry."

She went to the window and looked over at the garage. When she spotted Magnus with the tools in his hand she smiled to herself. He looked so meek, so meek and sad, and he needed her so much.

The moment he came through the door he asked whether the specialist had called. Although she had been prepared for the question she was at a loss for words.

"No," she said. "He hasn't called."

They ate early. The sun was still shining in the garden, its evening rays as warm and gentle as the light in Lartigue's photographs. She drew his attention to a nest at the top of a rowan tree and to the flowers she had planted that spring that were now in full bloom.

A change of weather had been forecast, and during the night the wind blew up and it started to rain. When they awoke in the morning there were big puddles in the garden, covered with leaves. And it wasn't even August.

august

Jakob wanted to go to the Canary Islands. They'd been there twice before and he had enjoyed himself. He showed Iris an advertisement from a travel agency featuring a photo of a white hotel with a large swimming pool separating the building from the beach. The travel agency was new and Jakob knew a man who had been on one of its beach holidays and recommended it. Jakob and he had chatted a bit about the hotel and the travel agency, agreeing that the agency was bound to offer better deals than its competitors while it was establishing itself. They also agreed that the rates would go up eventually so there was no reason to wait.

Jakob told this to Iris when he showed her the ad. He also pointed out that the hotel was off the beaten track. Although only a small section of beach was visible in the picture, there seemed to be fewer people on it than they were accustomed to encountering on their vacations. The hotel had only six floors, and the advertisement said the apartments were spacious and rooms with a beach view were still available. The latter were more expensive, but the difference was reasonable. Although Jakob would have liked to call the travel agency there and then to reserve a room with a balcony and a view, he knew it would be wiser to let Iris decide. Not to imply that she was the boss, but after twenty years Jakob knew it was better to include her in any plans. She was more cautious than he was, and he admitted it. She looked at the picture in the ad and asked a few questions before changing the subject. This did not surprise Jakob, as she had hinted that she would rather visit museums this year than go on another beach holiday. She had taken a course in archeology over the winter, so culture was uppermost in her mind. Sun, heat and sea breezes were uppermost in Jakob's. He needed a rest after months of unusually hard work. He was a carpenter, and the company he part owned had taken on many projects over the past year—too many in Iris's opinion. But everything had turned out well in the end, and they were able to make deadlines, though the pressure had been intense. Iris worked for the government, where life was easier.

As usual they compromised. Actually it was Iris's suggestion and Jakob agreed, though he was already fantasizing about the Canaries—the beach, the balcony overlooking it, the pool, the sea, the sky. Iris put her case in such a way that he couldn't avoid acquiescing. He thought it safest to do so with a smile so she wouldn't start asking what reservations he could possibly have. Of course he could have found a way out of his predicament, but he would rather not take the risk. He had never liked lying.

Iris proposed that they go to Slovenia. She had done her homework, gone on the Internet, borrowed books from the library, talked to a woman she worked with who had gone there last year, called the new travel agency that Jakob was sure was so superior and interrogated the man who answered the phone. Everyone agreed that it was paradise, she said. The hotel she had her eye on was on Lake Bled, where you could swim, go boating and fish or just lie on the bank and soak up the sun and fresh air. She quoted articles claiming that nowhere in Europe was the air as wholesome as it was south of the Alps. She told him too that the hotel used to be Tito's summer residence, and the man at the travel agency recommended it unreservedly, describing it as a historic building with furnishings untouched since the head of state used to stay there, deliberating on international affairs. As you can imagine, no cost was spared, he had said.

Finally she said what Jakob had been dreading she would say since she began her speech: "And it'll be so nice for you to go back there after all these years."

He had spent a whole winter in the former Yugoslavia when he was twenty. He had quit high school in his third year and switched to the Technical College, so he ended up graduating later than his age group. He had never regretted this decision because he had always known that he was not suited for so-called higher education. He was good with his hands and had begun making things with his father, who was also a carpenter and head of his union. It was his father who got him the job in Yugoslavia. He had connections through the union and had visited Yugoslavia once for a conference and twice on summer holidays. He said Yugoslavia was a model country and admired Tito.

Jakob had accepted the offer, though he and Iris had started dating by that time. They had met in high school but parted when Jakob left and went to the Tech. They met again at a mutual friend's party when their class graduated. Jakob thought Iris so beautiful in her graduation cap that he could think of little else for the next several days. She had always liked him and found him handsome, so he had no trouble catching her eye. It wasn't long before their names were linked; their friends said: "Jakob and Iris" or "Iris and Jakob" when they were invited to parties; it was as if things had always been like that and they no longer existed separately.

Some of their friends were going abroad to study, and Jakob's father suspected that although his son was in love and content in his job, he might wonder if he was missing something when he watched his friends heading out into the world. His father knew from his own experience that thoughts like these could make trouble later on. By autumn he had gotten Jakob a job in Ljubljana. Jakob was pleased, and Iris didn't object to the plan, although of course she knew she would miss him. She drove him to the airport, and they held each other for a long time before saying good-bye. She cried on the way back to town but had more or less recovered by the time she got home. Over the next months she concentrated on work and threw all her energy into her swimming.

Jakob enjoyed Ljubljana. There was plenty to do, and winter arrived later than at home in Iceland. On weekends he sometimes borrowed the foreman's car and drove down to the Adriatic, either alone or with one of his mates. In the evenings he played soccer or drank a few beers at a bar. He read a bit. He wrote to Iris weekly. She wrote to him more often.

Once the novelty had worn off he was lonely. The weather turned cold, and there were no more trips to the beach. He found his workmates sloppy but was in no position to complain. Some of them resented him for being too thorough. Although things never came to a head, he sensed a change in their attitude toward him. The invitations to soccer began to dry up, and trips to the bar became rare. He missed Iceland.

It was December when he met Anna. She worked at a little hotel downtown where he sometimes went for breakfast on weekends. Business was relatively quiet in winter, and they had a chance to talk. She was cheerful and friendly and reminded him a little of Iris, so he invited her to the movies. It was pouring when they met in front of the cinema, but by the time the film was over the rain had stopped. They had a beer at a café in the street where he lived and then spent the night together.

He had never meant for this to happen and was tortured by guilt the next day. But he recovered. Before he knew it he had begun to spend most evenings with Anna. She was quick to smile, merry and easygoing, and he slept better with her beside him and missed her when she was not there. The scent of her hair clung to his pillow, the same as the scent of Iris's hair. This lessened his guilt, strange as it may seem.

He and Iris had planned that she would visit him at Christmas, but he no longer wanted her to and suggested that they meet in Venice instead. There they spent a happy time together, and years later when things were tough Iris often said that she was buoyed by the memory of those days. She had always been fond of Jakob, but it was not until Venice that her feelings had deepened into love.

Jakob drove Iris to the airport, and they parted with an even bigger lump in their throats than in the autumn. When he got back to Ljubljana he swore that he would end his relationship with Anna. Naturally he had never told her about Iris, but he decided to do so; he would explain his mistakes to her and beg her forgiveness. He practiced in front of the mirror in his room, then invited her to the cinema, thinking it would be easier to tell her in the dark. He turned up twenty minutes before the film began and waited on the sidewalk outside. He was nervous, and when he saw her come around the corner he knew he wouldn't be able to hurt her. Her face lit up in one big smile when she spotted him, and breaking into a run she leaped into his arms. They spent the night together, and the moon shone in through his window.

Spring came early. The cherry trees in the center of town blossomed and the streams flowed from the mountains. Jakob had always planned to go home in the spring and looked forward to it. He didn't regret having spent the winter abroad but felt that the time away had only confirmed where his roots lay. He and Anna were still seeing each other, but he was trying to reduce the amount of time they spent together. His plan was succeeding, though more because of what was going on with her than because of anything he was doing. Her grandmother who lived near Lake Bled had fallen ill in early March, and she had to look after her, so she was in town only on weekends. Her family seemed close-knit; her parents lived near her grandmother, and her sister was in the same neighborhood. Anna had frequently invited Jakob to visit Lake Bled, but he had wriggled out of it. "Don't you want to meet my family?" she asked. He didn't like her tone. It dawned on him that her ideas about the future were probably quite different from his.

He didn't tell her he was leaving and didn't have the strength to say good-bye. He left on a Tuesday. They had spent the weekend together, and he began to prepare for his departure Monday morning as soon as he had taken her to the bus. He hadn't accumulated much stuff over the winter, so it didn't take long to pack. He wrote her a letter, taking a great deal of care because he wanted to be sure she couldn't use it against him. The letter contained no protestations of love, only gratitude for having known her. When he read it over he was ashamed and threw it in the bin.

He had two photos of Anna. In one she was alone; in the other she was with him. He had his arm around her and they were smiling at the camera; there was a cherry tree in the background. He threw that photo away after some thought but took the other one with him.

Back in Iceland he worried. The woman who had rented him the room in Ljubljana had taken his address so she could write to him, and he was afraid she would pass it on to Anna. He even imagined that Anna might come to look for him, and he was on his guard for the first few weeks. But the feeling passed, and by the time summer had arrived and he and Iris were engaged he had almost stopped thinking about Anna. The few times his thoughts strayed to her he felt guilty. So he tried to think of her as little as possible.

He never heard from Anna, and when his daughter was born and Iris suggested christening her Anna after her mother, he agreed without comment. After their son was born they moved into a new flat that looked out over the bay. He found the photo of Anna during the move, and instead of throwing it away he hid it in a book of old Nordic poems that he and Iris had received as a wedding present from her grandparents.

Their children were now around twenty and no longer felt like going on holiday with their parents, so Iris suggested asking their friends Philip and Hillary whether they would like to come along instead. Hillary worked for a well-known genetics company and had become Iris's best friend since she and Philip had come over from England. Jakob and Philip got on well. On the plane Hillary asked Jakob what he had found most memorable about his stay in Yugoslavia. Jakob answered that it was all so long ago he couldn't remember anything in particular. He also mentioned that he hadn't gone to Bled the winter that he had lived in Ljubljana, although he had often meant to. "I was always working," he said.

The hotel was magnificent, with walls of white marble, life-size statues and countless photographs of Tito and his guests. Iris recognized Haile Selassie, Khrushchev, Nehru, Akihito of Japan and Kim Il Sung from North Korea. The furniture was from the 1950s, and Iris and Hillary raved about how authentic everything was, as they put it. The hotel room faced the beach, and Iris opened the window before unpacking their bags. There were boats on the lake, and Jakob leaned out the window to watch them. Although he found the furniture ugly and the chair by the window where he had perched uncomfortable, he chose to agree with Iris when she admired the hotel and its surroundings.

"Apparently there are over a hundred different kinds of trees in the grounds here," she said.

They ate lunch on the veranda, and then Iris suggested that they all take a stroll by the lake. What Jakob wanted more than anything else was to stretch out on a lounge chair by the water with a cold beer, but he decided to join them anyway. He had been on edge since they arrived and blamed work. His father had once pushed himself too hard and been forced to take a long break. Jakob had been a teenager at the time and had found it strange to see his father in bed day after day.

They walked a long way and by evening Jakob was tired and went to bed before the others. He found the mattress too hard and slept badly.

The next day they bicycled around the area, and on the third day they planned to take a boat out on the lake. Iris, Hillary and Philip were ready by ten, but Jakob said he wanted a rest. "It'll do him good," Iris told Hillary and Philip. "He's had far too much on his plate recently."

Jakob reclined on a lounge chair down by the lake. A member of the hotel staff spread a white towel on the chair for him and asked whether he could bring him some fruit juice. Jakob accepted, and when he had finished his juice he dozed on the chaise longue. A breeze stirred the leaves in the gardens and the rustling relaxed him. He had watched Iris, Hillary and Philip row away from shore but lost sight of them some time ago. They were going to eat at a restaurant on the opposite shore and didn't expect to be back till late.

By one o'clock he was hungry. There were some tables down by the lake, served by waiters from the hotel, one of whom showed him to a seat, put up the umbrella and handed him the menu. Jakob took off his sunglasses but the glare from the water was fierce so he put them back on again. He waited for the waitress he had spotted in the distance to come over.

He was gazing out at the water when she arrived at his table, so he didn't notice her until she greeted him. He looked up but was quick to bury his face in the menu again. He hadn't paid the menu much attention and now hastily ordered the first thing he saw, omelet and salad. She asked what he would like to drink. Beer, he said. He handed her the menu, keeping his eyes lowered. It wasn't until she had set off back to the hotel that he dared look up.

He wasn't sure. It had been more than two decades ago. He hadn't looked at the picture of Anna for years, so he had to trust his memory, which he knew was no longer reliable. "It can't be her," he told himself; coincidences like that happen only in movies.

He followed her out of the corner of his eye as she came down the path from the hotel carrying the tray. Her age was right and her face was familiar, and so was the way she walked. He tried to recall Anna as she had looked twenty years ago but couldn't. In his memory she looked like the waitress.

He avoided meeting her eyes when she placed the omelet and beer on his table, and inadvertently disguised his voice when he thanked her. He didn't realize what he was doing until afterward and was ashamed of his foolishness. The beer was welcome, and by the time he finished the glass he had convinced himself that he had imagined the whole thing and decided to behave like a normal human being when she returned. There were sailboats out on the water. The wind had dropped, and the boats weren't moving. Yet he liked watching them becalmed and was aware of being more at peace than he had been for a long time.

He ordered another beer when she came to clear the plates from the table. Steeling himself, he looked up and smiled, but his smile vanished as their eyes met. He was sure that she recognized him. Her eyes convinced him, though Anna's happiness and candor had gone. He hung his head again, waiting for her to say something. He felt she was studying him as she took his side plate and stacked it on top of the plate with the omelet, cutlery and empty beer glass. She was in no rush. Her movements were sure and unhurried, as when she had served him for the first time at the hotel in Ljubljana.

When he was silent that evening Iris asked whether he was all right. They dined on the veranda, and Iris, Philip and Hillary talked of their day on the water. It had been a successful trip, and they agreed that the restaurant where they had had lunch had been very good, though Philip stressed that they had missed Jakob. They had also rowed out to the island in the lake and gone ashore. There was an old church there, and tourists were told that it was supposed to be good luck to ring the bells. There was a line but they all took turns.

"I did it twice," said Iris. "Once for me and once for you."

Jakob thanked her. He kept an eye out, but the waitress was nowhere to be seen. While they ate salad and fish Iris quoted the guidebook, which praised the hotel for its wholesome cooking. Jakob wouldn't have minded a hamburger but there weren't any on the menu. They looked out at the lake in the dusk and at the lights on the other side of the water once darkness had fallen. At any other time it would have seemed a perfect summer vacation evening, and Jakob was upset with himself for not being able to enjoy it. He said little, listening with only half an ear. Philip, on the other hand, was in top form after their outing and unusually talkative. Afterward Jakob couldn't remember how the conversation had turned to illnesses, and he found it strange how badly it affected him. It was Philip who started it by commenting on how many people in their age group were dying.

"Two funerals in the last couple of months," he said. "One cancer, the other a heart attack. Men in their prime."

"One of the women I work with is seriously ill," said Hillary. "A mother of three."

Iris said that a cousin of hers had died last Christmas at forty-eight.

"Imagine," they said.

Jakob was relieved when they finally got up. In bed his thoughts strayed to the Canary Islands. He had always been happy there.

The following day he joined them on a trip to the mountains and then suggested they eat somewhere other than the hotel that evening. They agreed. Iris was relieved when he cheered up during dinner. He drank a little red wine with the meal, and by the time they walked out into the sultry dusk he had begun to convince himself that the waitress couldn't be Anna. He slept better and the next day played a round of golf with Philip. That evening they dined at the hotel. Jakob had a drink with Philip down by the lake while their wives were getting ready. Jakob was in a good mood as they sat down. When he saw the waitress approaching the table he started a little but no one noticed.

The day before her hair had been loose but now it was tied back in a bun on her neck. He studied her as she answered some questions Iris had about the food; he was listening to her voice and trying to remember how Anna had sounded. But he couldn't recall. He tried yet again to summon up a picture of Anna in his mind but was no more successful than before.

He kept his cool as they ordered, although he felt the waitress was short with him, and he found her gaze uncomfortable. He had had a gin and tonic with Philip while they were waiting for their wives, and now he decided to have another. Philip went over the highlights of their golf game and praised the course. Iris and Hillary, who had visited a historic village near the lake, had much to say about their experience. Iris had started reminiscing about old times when the waitress brought the starter.

"Jakob, shouldn't we go to Ljubljana?" Iris asked. "Since we're here. Don't you think it would be fun?"

The waitress put the starter on the table in front of Hillary.

"There's not much to see there," he said.

"We could go just the two of us. It might not interest you," Iris said to Philip and Hillary, "but I never got there. We met in Venice instead."

"Venice is so romantic," said Hillary. "But we'd be quite happy to come along. Wouldn't we, Philip?"

"Yes, absolutely," he said.

Jakob had ordered soup. When the waitress brought his bowl it slipped in her hands. Several drops spilled on the table and onto the napkin in Jakob's lap. She apologized. Jakob thought it was a signal.

Philip had also ordered soup. The waitress placed bread on the plate beside his bowl but forgot to give Jakob any. Philip noticed this.

"First she splashes you, then she forgets your bread," he said. "What on earth have you done to her?"

Philip laughed and the women joined in. Jakob tried with difficulty to smile.

They talked about Tito and the cold war, and from there the conversation moved on to nuclear weapons. Philip had recently been reading about them. He knew exactly how many missiles the Americans and Russians had destroyed in recent years and how many they had left. He mentioned how badly the Russians guarded their weapons and prophesied that some nutcracker would get hold of one sooner or later. "It's a question of probability," he said. "Then the shit will really hit the fan."

Iris and Philip ordered trout for their main course, Jakob and Hillary veal. The veal came with mushrooms, leeks and gravy. Jakob thought the meat tasted lousy.

He woke at three in the morning with a stomach cramp. He tried to go back to sleep, but the pain grew worse and finally he had to go to the bathroom. When he threw up Iris came and tended to him. She wet a cloth and wiped his forehead, asking what he thought it was. He had an idea but kept quiet about it. After they got back into bed, Iris fell asleep but he lay awake. At five he visited the bathroom again. And again at seven. Then, exhausted and aching, he slept till midday.

There was a note on his bedside table when he opened his eyes. "Call me on my cell phone when you wake up," it said. He rang and asked Iris whether Hillary or Philip was sick. Philip had eaten soup like him, and Hillary the veal. Iris said they were in the best of health; they had gone for a walk in the morning and were now swimming in the lake.

"Oh," he said.

"How do you feel?" she asked.

"Shitty," he said.

She laughed. "At least you've got your sense of humor back."

He hadn't intended to be funny but let it go.

He was running a high fever and couldn't control his thoughts. He was now convinced that the waitress was Anna. He suspected that she had put something in his veal. Yet it bothered him that however hard he tried he couldn't picture how she had looked when they had known each other. He thought about the photo in the book of Nordic verse, and by four he had decided he needed to get hold of it. They were going to be another week at the hotel, and he was sure he couldn't bear to remain in this state of uncertainty. He argued back and forth with himself, declaring that he must have lost his mind to think she had poisoned him, urging himself to ask the woman straight out what her name was.

But he knew he couldn't do it, and neither did he feel he could ask any of the other staff. It was ridiculous, and word would get around; she would find out. Stumbling out of bed, he went over to the window and opened it. He was dizzy and had a hard time concentrating. But then he made up his mind all of a sudden, phoned his brother who had a key to the house and asked him to get the photo and send it to him by express mail. He urged him to make sure the kids weren't home because they mustn't know what he was up to. His brother asked what was going on. Who was this photo of, and why did Jakob need it all of a sudden?

"I'll tell you later," said Jakob. "Try to get it in the mail before this evening."

"Are you all right?" asked his brother.

"No," said Jakob. "I'm not feeling good."

He had no appetite, and Iris asked if she should spend the evening with him. He wouldn't hear of it, telling her he just needed to rest. When she had gone he phoned his brother and asked if he had sent the picture. His brother said yes; it was on its way and Jakob could expect it in the next couple of days.

"It wasn't cheap," he said.

"Doesn't matter," said Jakob.

He got up the next day but was careful not to overdo it. He had toast and tea for breakfast. The four of them walked along the lake in the morning and ate lunch in a little village not far from the hotel. In the afternoon they lay on lounge chairs on the beach. In the evening they went out to dinner. Jakob was relieved that Philip didn't bring up the subject of death or destruction.

Jakob had intended to contrive that Iris, Philip and Hillary would go on an excursion together the day the envelope arrived with the photo, while he stayed behind at the hotel. He had thought of suggesting a trip to the mountain villages because Iris had been reading about them and Philip and Hillary had listened with interest when she described their history. He himself would need to rest. He went to bed certain that this stratagem would work, and no doubt he would have been proved right had things gone according to plan.

He woke in a terrible state at two in the morning and spent the rest of the night vomiting. Iris decided to call a doctor. The doctor arrived promptly, gave Jakob a thorough examination and then advised him to rest. He didn't know what it was, but guessed probably a virus or food poisoning.

"What kind of poisoning?" asked Jakob. "I was better yesterday. What kind of poisoning keeps recurring?"

"It's probably a virus," the doctor said and took his leave.

Iris left the room with him. Jakob went to the bathroom and threw up. On his way back to bed he paused by the open window. He heard voices, soft laughter, the clattering of cutlery and plates. He looked out. On the veranda staff were preparing for lunch, setting tables, opening umbrellas, sweeping and cleaning. He spotted the waitress immediately, her arms full of white linen tablecloths and napkins.

"Natalya," called her colleague. "Here."

The waitress looked up, then walked over to the girl who had called for her and handed her a tablecloth and some napkins. They exchanged a few words, laughed then continued their work. Natalya . . .

Jakob went back to bed. Iris returned.

"He thinks you'll be better by tomorrow," she said. "You just have to rest."

"You should leave," he said. "I don't want to ruin your day."

But she wouldn't listen, and he fell asleep exhausted and depressed.

The mail arrived just after midday. There was a knock on the door, and Iris opened it. Jakob had been asleep, but now he stirred and opened his eyes. He closed them again immediately, however, when he saw Iris in the doorway.

"What was I thinking?" he said to himself. "What on earth was I thinking?"

She didn't open the envelope, nor did she wake him. She placed it on a round table by the window. Jakob lay still for a long time, pretending to be asleep while he wondered how to explain the letter. Iris either sat by the bed or walked around the room; from time to time she went to the window and looked out at the brilliant sunshine. When he thought she wasn't looking he half opened his eyes. Once he saw her standing by the table, inspecting the envelope. To Jakob Kristjansson, it said. From Kristjan Kristjansson. She picked it up and fingered it thoughtfully before putting it down again.

Unable to come up with a convincing explanation for the picture, he thought of asking Iris to go down and fetch him an orange juice. In the meantime he would open the envelope and put something else inside instead of the photo. But he had nothing that would seem even remotely plausible, and he soon abandoned these thoughts and acknowledged that he was no good at deceiving people.

When he rose up a little he saw that the sun was shining on the envelope.

"How are you?" she asked.

His stomach felt much better but he wasn't lying when he answered: "Not good."

He was careful to pretend not to notice the envelope, and she was quiet about it at first. Going into the bathroom, he splashed water on his face and brushed his teeth. Although he was still tanned, there were shadows under his eyes, his cheeks seemed to sag and his lips were dry.

She was standing by the window when he came out. She asked if she could do anything for him.

"No," he said, crawling back into bed. "You should just go out. I'm bound to get better if I rest."

"A letter came for you while you were asleep," she said.

"Really?" he said.

"From your brother. Do you know what it is?"

"It can't be anything important. What are Philip and Hillary doing?"

"They were going to relax on the beach."

"You should go and join them instead of hanging around here."

"Hasn't your brother been in touch with you about this letter?"

He closed his eyes. They should have gone to the Canaries. He should have told her that was what he wanted to do, that they could go somewhere else next year. He shouldn't have given in, not this time.

He told her everything. His account was not very coherent, and she was silent while he talked. He would have liked for her to say something, and sometimes he paused in his story to give her a chance, but it didn't work. He spoke about the poisoning and even tried to make her feel sorry for him but failed, and silence swallowed his words.

While he was talking he saw that his life was falling apart. He knew her so well, could read her thoughts, heard her say to herself: "It was all built on sand." He fell silent, breaking off in mid-sentence, unable to continue.

Everything was spoiled. Even the Venice trip was ruined. Iris would assume that Anna had lived in their home all these years, both in the book of Nordic poems given to them by her grandparents for a wedding present and, more important, in Jakob's heart. He was about to respond to her unspoken thoughts, about to say, "I'd forgotten all about that photo; it's ages since I've looked at it," but he had the sense to keep quiet. "How long?" he imagined her asking. "When was the last time you looked at it?"

She stood by the foot of the bed, watching him as he talked. He avoided her eyes, staring either up at the ceiling or to the side. When he fell silent he took a deep breath, wiped his brow and summoned the courage to look at her.

With one hand on her hip, she was studying him carefully. When she finally spoke, her voice indicated that she was in deep thought.

"Express mail," she said. "How much did that cost?"

He didn't know what to say, and she didn't wait for an answer.

"You really need to rest, darling. This virus is clearly more serious than I thought."

She wet a towel and put it on his forehead. He lay still, listening to the echo of the church bells ringing ceaselessly in the quiet afternoon.

september

When Edda went abroad to study, her mother gave her a warning. They had said their good-byes and were standing side by side in front of passport control when her mother lowered her voice and said: "For God's sake, Edda dear, don't get involved with an American. Whatever you do, just not an American."

Her mother didn't usually try to influence her. There really wasn't any need; Edda had always been a good girl, diligent and stable. Her mother's words took her by surprise. She turned to her without answering and looked at her as if to be sure she hadn't misheard, at which her mother added in explanation: "It always ends badly. You remember what happened to my cousin Svana."

They said good-bye again, more fondly than before, and Edda looked back and smiled while her passport was being checked. Her mother, who was still standing in the same spot, waved to her, trying to smile back, but the anxiety in her mother's face lingered in Edda's memory along with the warning.

That had been a beautiful fall day a decade ago, perhaps to the day, for September had come again and her thoughts were of autumn, although the days were still hot and the trees in full leaf. Usually she would have enjoyed these September days, heading into Central Park when she had finished work, walking around the reservoir or just sitting under a tree with a book or magazine, listening to the birds and the afternoon sounds of the city. That's what she would have done if things had been all right; she might even have bought fruit and sandwiches on the way, called Mark and asked him to join her. Perhaps he would have had time, perhaps not, but she would have enjoyed the visit to the park either way and wouldn't have gone home till dusk.

Recently, however, she had been too restless to sit on a bench and listen to birdsong. Her marriage to Mark was hanging by a thread. As her friend Katrin, who was married to the Icelandic cultural attaché, had said to her, the most obvious solution would be for her to end it. Edda had long known that little was left of her marriage, but it was only now that she was facing the fact. She was patient and discreet by nature, wanted the best for everyone and couldn't bear to see anyone suffer; maybe that was why she had put up with Mark all these years. Sometimes she even wondered whether she had ever loved him. She felt guilty when she thought this way, and blamed herself for letting herself be talked into marrying him. Admittedly, he had pursued her single-mindedly, but she was sure he would have been better off if he had met a woman who loved him as he deserved. She didn't. Not anymore, anyway. She felt he had changed; there were cracks in his self-confidence, the quality she had probably been most attracted to initially. He had always been so cocky, dismissing all doubts, acting as if nothing could stand in his way. When things were going well for him she had persuaded herself that his hubris had a foundation.

She was proper and a bit old-fashioned, and found it difficult to admit that sex had played an important part in their relationship.

She had been raised by religious parents, and while she was able to joke about their ways, the upbringing had still left its mark. Before she had met her husband she had had only one lover, whom she was quick to forget.

She and Mark had met shortly after she finished her degree. She had studied design and taken a job in New York with a company that published fashion magazines. She meant to work there for six months to gain experience before going home to Iceland, where she had good prospects for a job with a television network. They had met at a fashion show. She was there for work; Mark had come with a friend, one of Edda's colleagues. They exchanged a few words, Mark doing most of the talking, but when the evening was over she forgot him. He did not forget her, however, and wouldn't stop calling her until she agreed to go out to dinner with him. Although she was beautiful she was unused to male attention. Her friends told her it was because men thought she wanted nothing to do with them. This was unfair. She was quiet and didn't waste words, and those who didn't know her often found it difficult to keep up a conversation with her. But Mark didn't let this deter him, accustomed as he was to selling stocks to people who weren't sure if they really needed them. Although he often went over the top, sending her flowers at work and so on, he charmed her with all the fuss. He was brisk and articulate, dressed well, tamed his thick hair in a tasteful style and wore glasses that made him look quite intelligent. When Edda discovered that the lenses were plain glass she didn't know what to think. They hadn't started living together at that stage, but he had recently proposed to her. She asked him why he wore glasses when he didn't need to. She looked serious, but he burst out laughing and asked why men wore ties. Then he did what he usually did when she frowned—kissed her on the cheek and tugged good-humoredly at the corners of her mouth to make her smile. He generally succeeded, but this time she remained pensive.

She was modest and quiet, he the life of the party. She preferred staying in after work; he could hardly bear to spend an evening in the apartment. "We're young," he said, "and the city has so much to offer. We can stay home when we're old." "Or when we have children?" she suggested. "Or when we have children," he agreed, but then added that it would be best for them to wait a few years. "We both need to establish ourselves," he said, "you no less than me."

She did well at work. She stayed at the same place and got raises from time to time but didn't ask for much responsibility. Mark, on the other hand, changed jobs frequently. He got himself noticed, spending his money as soon as he earned it. When Edda asked why he bought such expensive watches, shoes and clothes and ate only at fancy restaurants, he told her that he was investing in his image. Those were his exact words, and she told herself that she didn't understand the rules of his business so it would be wrong of her to argue with him.

The economy was booming during the first years of their marriage, and the shares Mark sold went up more often than not. He was forever on the go, whereas she generally stayed home in the evenings, sometimes falling asleep before he got in. For two summers in a row he rented a beach house in the Hamptons where they spent weekends and their summer vacation. She got three weeks off; he seemed to have free rein—after all, he was always working, as he said himself. He knew many people who owned summerhouses in the area, and he attended parties diligently. Though Edda tried to get out of some of them, it wasn't as easy as in the city. The rent in the Hamptons was not cheap, but she didn't complain because Mark pointed out that many of the people they socialized with were his clients. Nor did she object when he bought an old convertible for use in the country. It was black with white seats. She had been planning to go to Iceland for both those summers but felt it would be imprudent financially now that he had rented the house and bought the convertible. Perhaps she could have allowed herself to go, but she was thrifty and felt they should use the house since they had paid for it.

He didn't tell her when he was fired. Before when he changed jobs he had always tried to take as many clients with him as he could and had never been able to relax, but she got up one Monday morning and he turned over and said he wanted more sleep. She called him on his cell phone at midday and asked what was going on. He said he was having lunch with a prospect and was brief. He gave the impression that things couldn't be better.

It didn't escape her that the boom was over and the stock market was no longer automatically going up. She had read about it in the papers but never heard Mark complain. He didn't complain when he lost his job either. He insisted that he had chosen to quit of his own accord because the company didn't meet either his or his clients' expectations. He said he was going to take a rain check for a few days before deciding his next step; there were plenty of options, and this time he wasn't going to rush into anything. It sounded sensible but Edda was still worried.

He kept to his customary habits: put on a suit when he got up, went to meetings, lunched with people he knew, visited old clients and saw contacts he thought might be useful. But Edda was sure he was in trouble. She had recently seen *Death of a Salesman* with her friend Katrin and felt as if she were observing Mark the whole time. Once she watched him standing in front of the mirror in his underpants, muttering something to himself. He didn't see her and she found herself feeling sorry for him because somehow she got the idea that at that moment he was being honest with himself. He was in good shape, exercised regularly and had never had a weight problem, yet somehow she found him so pitiful that she wanted to do anything to help him.

When he noticed she was standing there she discovered how mistaken she had been.

"Honey," he said, "is that a gray hair?"

"What?"

"There," he said, gesturing without taking his eyes off the mirror.

"I can't see anything," she said.

"Maybe it's just the light," he said. "Dad didn't start going gray till he was fifty."

As she walked away, he added: "I've started my own company. I'm putting up some money myself, but most of it is coming from others. I think the Hoffmanns will invest. Things are looking good."

"Putting up money yourself?" she repeated. "We can't afford it."

He smiled as men smile at children.

"Don't worry. I took a loan. Everyone wants to be in on this."

Edda knew she was more careful with money than most, so she hesitated to form an opinion of his plans. Economy and thrift had been a part of her upbringing. She clearly remembered her father's reaction when he heard that her brother had mortgaged his house. "Perhaps this is okay," she told herself; "perhaps that's how business is done." But however she tried to persuade herself, she always came to the same conclusion: she didn't trust Mark; she anticipated mistakes and disappointments. Maybe he sensed this, maybe not. But he was away more than usual, and when she asked how things were going he cut the conversation short or said: "As well as they possibly could, though I know you don't believe me." She was ashamed and asked herself yet again whether she was being unfair to him.

In June he suddenly began to talk about having a baby. She was shocked because she had been about to tell him that she thought it would be most sensible for them to separate. She arranged to meet her friend Katrin at a café and confided in her about her dilemma. Katrin was able to convince her that it would be a terrible mistake for her to get pregnant. Edda told her that at times she felt as if she was failing Mark. Katrin said she should face facts. "You don't love him," she said. "You feel sorry for him. What kind of marriage is that? And don't forget you're thirty. It's one thing to be twenty-five, another to be thirty. It's tough out there. Just be grateful you don't have children."

Katrin suggested that she and Edda go to Paris in September. She and her husband had been based there before they came to New York and had made many friends. They often reminisced about their time in France, raving about everything French—the food, culture, clothes, language and aesthetic sense—and sometimes spoke French to each other, especially when they had had some wine. Katrin had confided in Edda that their sex life was never better than when they did it in French. Even though Edda regarded this as too much information she sometimes caught herself thinking about it.

Katrin had arranged to borrow an apartment from her friend Clemance, who would be away in China. Since her husband had decided to go salmon fishing in Iceland, Katrin thought it would be a perfect opportunity for her and Edda to spend a week together in Paris.

"You need it," she said. "After everything you've been through."

The apartment was located on a quiet little street not far from Pont Neuf, and Clemance had no objections to her inviting Edda along; there were two spacious bedrooms in the flat.

By the time they left the café Edda had promised to tell Mark that she thought it would be unwise for them to have children as things stood, and to inform him about the Paris trip at the same time.

Perhaps Mark had sensed what was coming. Edda couldn't explain it otherwise. He came home with flowers for her, and when she looked at them in their vase on the living room table she asked herself why she was such a pushover. He brought up children again. She knew he was manipulating her, but that didn't change anything. She was confused and finally stammered that they should wait and see. She felt almost ashamed when she added that she was going to Paris with Katrin in September.

Knowing he had dodged a bullet, he encouraged her to go to Paris. He bragged about the company he had set up, claiming that by fall everything would be in full swing, so he wouldn't be able to join her anyway.

Over the next few weeks she overheard him talking on his cell phone about his new business, and although he tried to take his conversations out of her earshot she suspected that the people who had lent him money were growing impatient. The Hoffmann family didn't seem in any hurry to invest in the company, and the clients he claimed he had made rich and who he expected would follow him into his new venture could not make a decision. Neither could Edda. In fact, she might have dithered forever if it hadn't been for the statue.

At the beginning of August he told her they had been invited out to Long Island for the weekend. They hadn't rented a house that summer, but friends of Mark's had a small guesthouse on their property, and he said they were keen for Mark and Edda to visit. This was the first she had heard of these people. When they pulled up to the house on a Friday evening it turned out the couple wasn't home. A housekeeper greeted them and showed them to the guesthouse; she said they had been expected but couldn't say when their hosts would be back. Mark was in high spirits. He told Edda they were filthy rich and had fingers in every pie. "They'll be here tomorrow," he said. "There's a charity dinner at the hotel tomorrow evening, and they've bought a table. We're invited."

He hadn't mentioned this dinner before, and Edda asked him to tell her more about it. He said he wasn't sure what the dinner was in support of but had a feeling it was either disabled children or the local library. "The Hoffmann family will be at the next table," he said.

"I don't have any clothes with me," she said. "Why didn't you tell me before we left?"

"Honey," he said, "we'll buy you something to wear. There are great stores here in town."

It was hot and humid and the clouds thickened toward the evening. The sky turned black and a thunderstorm broke out. Feeling tired, they lay side by side in the big bed in the guesthouse with the window open, listening to the rain. He reached for her hand, and she opened her palm and they clasped fingers as thunder shook the house and raindrops rattled on the patio outside.

"I know it's been a hard time for you," he said quietly. "It's been hard for me too. But everything's coming together now. Finally."

He had never spoken like this before, and she was intensely relieved to know that he hadn't completely lost touch with reality. She squeezed his hand unconsciously, and soon they were making love. It had been a long time and they were both a little awkward at first. But they got over it. Afterward, as they were drifting off to sleep, she told herself that maybe it wasn't too late for them to put right what had gone wrong.

She bought a dress in Southampton the next morning, and later they ate lunch outdoors at a little restaurant in Sag Harbor. There were sailboats in the bay and gulls soaring over the beach, and she felt better than she had for a long time. She read a book she had brought along while Mark read the paper, and when the meal was over they drank espresso from tiny cups. Later they took a stroll along the beach, and when they came home their hosts, the Schwartzmans, had arrived. They welcomed them, and Mrs. Schwartzman asked Edda whether she was looking forward to the evening. It transpired that the charity dinner was in aid of the deaf.

"We'll meet at six," said Mrs. Schwartzman, "and have a drink before we go. Are you comfortable in the guesthouse?"

At six Edda and Mark walked across the lawn to the main house. The veranda doors were open and they heard music from inside. Their hosts welcomed them, and the man asked Mark how he was doing with the new company.

"Great," said Mark, "it's all coming together. I think the Hoffmanns are finally in."

"Congratulations," said Mr. Schwartzman. "Good for you. They're tightfisted sons of bitches."

"They haven't signed yet," said Mark, "but I talked to their lawyer yesterday and he said we were practically there."

"Be careful," said Mr. Schwartzman. "I know Harry Hoffmann well. He can't be trusted."

As they drank cocktails out on the veranda, the sun sank in the sky and the lawn took on a blue shade in the afternoon light. Mrs. Schwartzman spent a lot of time on the phone while Mark and her husband talked business. Edda didn't mind.

The dinner began at seven. It was crowded. Edda knew no one. Mark was acquainted with lots of people, however, and exchanged small talk. She found him too ingratiating, but that was nothing new. He kissed the women on the cheek and shook the men's hands, slapping them on the shoulder and telling them they looked well. She couldn't help sensing, as she had so often before, that although people were friendly to him they regarded him as a lightweight. That was the word she used to herself. "Lightweight." She couldn't help it.

At half past seven the signal came for the dinner guests to take their seats. There were name cards by the places on the large round tables. There were nine at their table; one person had dropped out. On Edda's right was a man who said he was a stockbroker; her host's brother sat on her left. He was a heavyset fellow and kept mopping the sweat off his brow with his white linen napkin.

The master of ceremonies welcomed the guests and thanked them for supporting a worthy cause. Keeping his speech short, he told two jokes before outlining the evening's program. There would be several speeches, Harry Hoffmann would be honored for his contribution to deaf causes, then there would be an auction of four works of art: three paintings and one statue. *"Bon appétit,"* he said before stepping down from the microphone.

The meal passed without incident. The speeches about deafness went in one ear and out the other. There was a great deal of talk at their table, and Edda's dinner partners both turned out to be congenial. The Hoffmann family sat with their friends and relatives at the table closest to the stage, and Mark went over to say hello. He asked Edda to come with him so he could introduce her, but she excused herself. She was embarrassed to see him fawning over these people.

Harry Hoffmann was short and slight and talked so loud when he spoke, thankful of the honor, that the microphone screeched. The host's brother leaned over to Edda and explained that Hoffmann was trying to be considerate to the many hard-of-hearing people in the audience. When Edda looked around she saw two elderly men at the next table struggling to turn down the volume on their hearing aids. Her father had a hearing aid, so she knew that loud noise only made matters worse.

" . . . And so I urge all of you to reach into your wallet," said Hoffmann in conclusion. "You'll have a chance to put your money where your mouth is later on this evening when the artworks are auctioned."

There was thunderous applause, and the serving staff started pouring coffee into cups and liqueurs into glasses. Mark got to his feet as he clapped. Edda was so embarrassed that she had to look away.

"Fantastic," said Mark as he sat down, "fantastic." He had drunk white wine with the starter and red wine with the main course and he was feeling the effects. He raised his liqueur glass and proposed that everyone at his table should toast Harry Hoffmann and, of course, their hosts.

The auctioneer was a professional. He began by praising the art, then urged people to be generous. "This is a good cause," he said repeatedly. There was a convivial atmosphere in the room, and the waiters followed orders and diligently topped up people's liqueur glasses. The first painting was of a house by a beach, and the host's brother claimed to have heard of the artist. He began to bid for it but dropped out when the price got too high. The second and third paintings were both landscapes. Edda was not impressed by either, but the auctioneer did his job. He stressed that the paintings were old, and the artists dead.

"Works like these only go up in value," he said.

Edda enjoyed watching the auction. The atmosphere in the room was competitive, and people took pleasure in raising their hands so as to be noticed, especially as the price escalated. There was a constant murmur in the room.

The auctioneer took a sip of water before the statue was put up for bidding. Now they had come to the high point of the evening, he claimed.

"Some of you may not know the sculptor," he said, "but he is famous and respected not only in his homeland, France, but in the international art world. Of course the most important consideration is that the statue is a gift from the Hoffmann family and has taken pride of place in their private collection for many years."

The dinner guests clapped and a few yelled bravo.

"Let's start the bidding at five thousand dollars," said the auctioneer.

"Do you know the sculptor?" the host's brother asked Edda. He had managed to extract from her that she had graduated from art school.

"No," she said, "but that doesn't mean anything. I don't know much about French sculptors."

There was a fight for the statue. The price rose swiftly. Although the statue wasn't clearly visible from farther back in the room, Edda thought it depicted a couple embracing. It was about a foot and a half high and ten inches wide. The auctioneer had lifted it with difficulty and said it was solid.

When the price reached twenty-eight thousand dollars the competition began to fall away. Two men carried on bidding but raised their offers slowly. Edda could see one of them, but the other was toward the back of the room. The auctioneer kept them to the mark. When the price had risen to $29,500, however, one of them dropped out, the one Edda couldn't see. She noticed that the other was smiling as he received his neighbors' compliments.

"We're so close to thirty thousand," said the auctioneer. "There must be someone here who is willing to offer thirty thousand dollars for this magnificent statue. A gift from the Hoffmann family, don't forget. From their private collection."

At that moment Edda's eyes went to Mark. He was on the edge of his seat, staring at the statue and Harry Hoffmann in turn. "No," she said aloud to herself, "oh no."

Afterward she asked herself whether she could have stopped him. He was sitting opposite her across the large table, so she would have had to either shout at him or get up and run around the table to silence him. It wouldn't have worked. There was no time. His hand was in the air within seconds.

"Thirty thousand!" shouted the auctioneer. "Gone to the young man at table four. Thirty thousand dollars!"

Mark received thanks and congratulations. Even Harry Hoffmann shook him by the hand. Mark was radiant but took care not to look in his wife's direction. She had the feeling some people were grinning. The host's brother nudged her and said: "Do you have a place in mind for it?"

They drove home with their hosts after the dinner, sitting in the back of their SUV. The statue was perched between them. They discussed the evening, and Mrs. Schwartzman praised Mark for his winning bid. Edda remained silent the whole way, even when they had returned to the guesthouse and were in bed. Mark tried to justify the purchase but quickly gave up. She remained silent the following day on the train back to New York. It was not until she met her friend Katrin after work on Monday that she found her tongue.

She didn't really talk much then either, but cried for the most part. Katrin said things had gone too far; Edda would have to do something. Edda said she knew. "I don't know whether I can cope with living alone," she stammered.

"You'll have to try," said Katrin. "This can't continue."

"When we get back from Paris," said Edda. "Maybe then. You can't imagine how much I'm looking forward to the trip."

The next weeks were difficult. Mark tried to placate her but gave up when he saw it wasn't working, and absented himself. He had until September to pay for the statue, and she decided not to ask him how he meant to do it. Once, in the middle of the night, she found him sitting in the living room, staring thoughtfully at the object. She went back to bed without letting him know she was there.

She tried Googling the sculptor but couldn't find him. It seemed strange, but she concluded that Mark hadn't spelled the name right. She left it at that because she had no intention of getting involved.

She went to see a therapist who told her nothing she didn't already know about her and Mark. Talking didn't help, and she found it just as difficult as before to take action. She felt she would be failing if she divorced him, though quite whom she would be failing she didn't know. No one in her family had been divorced, neither her parents nor her brothers or sisters. She would be the first. Apart from cousin Svala, who had married a man from the American base.

She was on her way home from work one evening when Katrin rang and told her she wouldn't be able to go to Paris; her mother had been suddenly taken ill and she needed to be by her side.

"But you must go," she said. "I won't hear of anything else."

Edda flew to Paris on Air France that Friday evening. The plane was due to depart at ten, and she made sure she came home late from work so she wouldn't have to talk to her husband more than necessary. She had packed her bags that morning and now asked the taxi to wait outside while she went upstairs to get them. Mark helped her down to the street with them, and she said good-bye to him with a hurried kiss on the cheek.

She dipped into a French dictionary for the first part of the journey and slept the rest of it. She drank a glass of white wine with her meal and decided to speak nothing but French during the trip. She had scored 9.5 out of 10 in French in high school and had tried to keep it up when she was at university. She was now determined to use this opportunity to refresh what she had forgotten and perhaps even improve what she knew.

Paris greeted her with blue skies and warm, still weather. It was only seven in the morning when she pulled up at the apartment on rue Christine. She paused before going inside, looked down the empty street. The sun had begun to shimmer on the stones of the sidewalk, and she sensed as she unpacked that the day would be hot.

She rested until eleven. The apartment was clean and bright and nicely furnished. Large windows opened out onto the street; there were plant containers on the broad windowsills, and after her nap she reached out and watered the flowers. Everything was quiet. She took a long shower before setting off into the city.

On the staircase she met a woman who lived on the floor above. *"Bonjour,"* the woman said and introduced herself.

"Bonjour," replied Edda. *"Je m'appelle Sif."*

She hadn't intended to introduce herself in this way. Admittedly her name was Edda Sif, but she never used her middle name. Yet now it fell so naturally from her lips that she couldn't help feeling there must be a reason. Perhaps it was a sign that she would turn over a new leaf on this trip. Begin a new life. To her surprise she felt ready all of a sudden.

The sun shone unceasingly those first days. She walked the length and breadth of the city, often sitting at tables outside cafés and enjoying a cold drink or perhaps a glass of white wine or rosé.

She went to bed early and rose early and tried to speak nothing but French, even to herself. She read a lot, visited museums and ate supper at small restaurants in the neighborhood. It was generally warm enough to sit outside, and she took a book with her to read by candlelight once darkness had fallen. She was content.

Katrin called after Edda had been in the city two days. They spoke French on the phone, and Katrin said she was madly envious of her. "What's it like being alone?" she asked after having reported on her mother's health.

"*C'est bon,*" replied Edda, and they both laughed heartily.

On the fifth day Mark called. Edda was annoyed at having to break her resolution and speak English. He was chatty, but she cut their conversation short after a few minutes. "My battery's low," she said. She had decided not to give him the phone number at the apartment.

After a week she had grown attached to a small restaurant in her neighborhood. The food was simple but delicious, the ingredients fresh. There were only ten tables inside and four in the garden. The owner, a man from Marseilles, not much older than she, made sure she always got the same table after she told him she liked it. It was in a corner of the garden under an old oak tree, a place that held on to the last embers of day after the sun had set. The owner, who was pleasant and polite, inquired when she dined solo at his place for the third time whether she was alone in the city. She had been late that evening, not dining until ten, and he took a seat at her table after the other guests had gone. They chatted for a while; he introduced himself as Antoine and drank a glass of wine with her. He was not at all pushy, so she accepted his offer to go with him to the vegetable market the following day. He said he would pick her up at ten, then bid her good-night.

He was punctual. She had gotten up early as usual and spent a long time getting ready, eventually choosing a yellow dress that she had always thought made her look happy. There were photographs of Clemance and other people all over the apartment and Edda studied them while she waited for him. She deduced that Clemance was an adventurous type, independent and self-confident. In one photo she was sitting on a camel in the desert. In another she was scaling a steep mountainside. They were interesting pictures, but Edda didn't dwell on them so much as on the pictures of Clemance in the company of men. There were a lot of them, particularly in the albums that Edda found in a cupboard under the bookshelves. Edda saw that Clemance evidently found it easy to be around men and enjoyed their company.

"Bonjour, Sif," Antoine said when she came out. "What a beautiful dress."

The day was a success, and when he delivered her home at five he asked whether she would come out to dinner with him. She agreed, and they kissed on both cheeks in parting. She took a bath and wondered what to do when the dinner was over.

They dined in the Latin Quarter. The restaurant was owned by a man from Marseilles like Antoine, and he gave them a royal welcome. Edda felt comfortable in Antoine's company; it was easy to talk to him and just as easy to be silent with him. They drank rosé and red wine, and after the meal had finished he reached for her hands and caressed them. By then it was past midnight.

When they arrived at her apartment she asked him to let the taxi go and come in with her. She had made up the bed before going out so it was ready for them. She turned down the lights and didn't feel uncomfortable about undressing in front of him. He was a gentle lover, and she discovered that there was a lot to what Katrin had said about French having a good effect on one's sex life.

They fell asleep after making love, and when Edda woke in the night it was raining. She put on a bathrobe, opened the window and stuck her head out. The raindrops were warm and she guessed it was a good-weather shower that would pass in a few hours. The glow of the streetlamps reached into the room and fell on the bed where Antoine was sleeping. She felt serene as she studied him, with no sense of remorse. That surprised her.

Antoine got up at six and dressed quietly. She was aware of him but carried on dozing. She felt good, and when he kissed her on the brow in parting she smiled without opening her eyes. *"Au revoir,"* he whispered.

The weather had cleared up by the time she awoke. It was nine o'clock. She hadn't slept that well in a long time. There were still raindrops on the petals of the flowers on the windowsill, but they evaporated when the sun came out. She drank her morning coffee down by the Seine. Antoine called her on her cell phone after midday and asked whether she would like to wander around with him. He said he was free for the next few hours and suggested they look at some secondhand stores; he needed an attractive clock for the lobby of his restaurant. They agreed to meet at Pont Neuf at one o'clock, and she ordered another cup of coffee and a pain au chocolat after they had rung off.

They went from one antiques store to another, but Antoine could find nothing he liked. He took his time, looking with no particular urgency, and seemed not really to care whether he was successful. Edda tried to help but was careful not to interfere. They walked hand in hand. Edda turned off her phone because she didn't want to be disturbed. They bought ice creams, sat on a bench in a little square and watched the world go by. Edda avoided the thought that she had a ticket booked for New York in three days.

It was she who suggested they go to a few more stores. She wanted to see if Antoine could find a serviceable clock because she thought he probably would have if she hadn't been there. Perhaps it was nonsense, but she assumed he would have been able to concentrate better. She had noticed a small side street while they were eating their ice creams, and now they walked down it hand in hand, looking in windows and going into the stores they liked the look of.

These were cheaper than the shops they had visited before but carried mostly replicas. Still, there was the odd object of interest lurking among the junk, and Edda almost bought a small mirror that she thought pretty.

She caught sight of the statues when she looked in the mirror. They were up on a shelf in the gloom at the back of the shop, five of them, side by side. She hesitated before turning around. "Is everything all right?" Antoine asked because her face had changed. Without answering him she walked over to the shelf at the back of the shop and stopped.

There was no difference between these and the statue Mark had paid thirty thousand dollars for. Each cost a hundred and twenty euros, but when the owner saw that Edda looked interested, she immediately dropped the price to a hundred. Antoine smiled as he watched Edda, assuming she would say something funny about these hideous things. But she took one of them down from the shelf in silence and held it for a while before putting it back. It was the same weight as the one Mark had bought, just as heavy, just as high and with the same mark on the base, a copy like his.

The lady repeated the offer without Edda's noticing. She was thinking of Mark, and to her great chagrin she now felt that she had failed him. She who had a degree in fine arts and could with a little effort have found out the truth about the statue. It wouldn't have required much work, but she had avoided getting involved, shrugging her shoulders when her search for the sculptor had been unsuccessful.

She tried to stem these thoughts, knowing they would lead to nothing but misery. She had always felt sorry for him, always felt involved in his misfortunes, just like a mother who feels responsible for her offspring's mistakes. She remembered how he had behaved at the auction and reminded herself that the statue had simply been the last straw.

She talked to herself this way, and much to her relief her arguments did not fall on stony soil. She imagined what Katrin would advise her to do. It didn't take her long to decide: Katrin would tell her to call Mark and explain to him that he had no choice but to confront Harry Hoffmann. She would tell her to force him to face up to his own failings and make it clear that she no longer felt she owed him anything; those days were over.

She gave a sigh of relief and Antoine must have noticed. He had been waiting, but now he laid his hand on her shoulder and said: "Surely you don't like them?"

"No," answered Edda, "they're ugly."

She was close to smiling, and if he hadn't added anything they would no doubt have left the shop hand in hand and continued their wandering, looking forward to meeting that evening at his restaurant, dreaming of the night to come. But instead of leaving it at that he continued: "That's putting it mildly. But I guess there are people who are stupid enough to buy them."

At these harmless words something burst inside Edda. She snatched one of the statues from the shelf, took it to the counter, reached with trembling fingers into her purse and put down a hundred and twenty euros.

The woman took the money in silence.

"Sif," said Antoine, "what's the matter? At least don't pay more than she asked for."

"Yes, I will," said Edda. "I'll pay the full price."

The assistant was going to wrap the statue and put it in a bag but she didn't have a chance because Edda left as soon as she had paid. She cradled the statue in her arms like a baby as she walked up the street, quickening her steps. The sun was low in the sky and blue shadows surrounded her, stretching up the walls of the houses. Yet ahead, in the square where they had sat on a bench eating ice cream, it was still bright. She hurried there as if in urgent need of the sunshine, not looking back. Antoine followed her; when he caught up she was standing quite still in the square, staring into space.

"What happened?" he asked. "What on earth happened?"

She didn't answer. She wanted to tell him, but she didn't have the strength to speak, nor to wipe away the tears that were pouring down her face quite against her will.

october

David arrived first. They had arranged to meet at six, and he had been lingering in a bookshop down the street to make sure he wasn't too early. It was now five past, and he was surprised Stefan wasn't already there. He had assumed Stefan wouldn't keep him waiting this time. Glancing around he decided not to sit down. There were not many customers in the café at this hour, as their friend Benedikt had predicted, mostly young people smoking and staring into space. It was Benedikt who had persuaded them to meet, pressing David until he gave in.

He was about to leave when he saw Stefan. He had a newspaper under his arm and looked quickly right and left before hurrying across the street. He cut a flamboyant figure as usual, his coattails flapping around him. As he strode into the café he ran a hand over his dark tangle of hair.

After they said their hellos Stefan took off his coat. It was new. They sat down and Stefan handed him the paper.

"There's a picture of you in here," he said. "Maybe you've seen it already?"

David hadn't. They got their pictures in the papers from time to time but didn't usually comment on the fact.

"Good picture," said Stefan. "Have you been waiting long?"

He was nervous, David could tell. He glanced around, running a hand through his hair again. His eyes rested briefly on a young woman sitting alone by the window, but then he seemed to realize that this was hardly the time for eyeing girls. He coughed. David waved to the waiter.

David ordered an espresso and after some hesitation Stefan followed suit. They put lemon zest in it, and Stefan asked the waiter for sugar. There were still a few cars on the street, shopworkers on their way home, idlers enjoying a leisurely drive in the good weather. It had been glorious for the past few days, beautiful fall weather with blue skies and light winds. Apart from the occasional night frost it was mild for the time of year.

They had been friends since their teens. Stefan was a year older than David, who had celebrated his thirty-fifth birthday two weeks ago. That was when everything had come unstuck. David had told Benedikt that he found this ironic: "Nice birthday present, don't you think?" he said. He and Stefan had met through Benedikt, who was older and had been in the business longer when the three of them first started playing together. In a newspaper review that they sometimes quoted, laughing, they had been described as a promising new act, making innovative music with "an upbeat rhythm and southern flavor." Benedikt played guitar, David piano and Stefan bass. Both David and Stefan sang. They were still popular and had adapted their music to the changing times as people do. They got plenty of gigs, earning enough from their music to feed and clothe themselves. Many regarded their lifestyle as enviable, and they were aware themselves that they were lucky, yet in their heart of hearts both undeniably felt they had failed to realize their potential.

They were talented and had early on gone on tour overseas, playing in Copenhagen and London, but despite good reception from audiences these tours hadn't led to anything. It was one thing to be twenty with world fame ahead, another to be thirty-five with dreams of fame behind them. But they didn't complain; they never let it show that they weren't as successful as they had hoped to be.

Benedikt had settled down years ago and had two children with his wife, Solveig. With David and Stefan it was a different story. They had always been accomplished womanizers. Opportunities came with the territory, and it didn't hurt that they were both good-looking. Benedikt had often been entertained in the early years by their stories of nocturnal adventures. There had always been an element of rivalry between them, in both music and love, but never enough to overshadow their friendship. In recent years, however, the stories had begun to tail off, and Benedikt suspected they no longer dived in with the same reckless abandon as before. Things had changed. Now it seemed as if their main motivation was to prove to themselves that women still found them attractive.

Stefan and David liked to party after their gigs, and Benedikt would remark that their night was just beginning when he went home to his wife and children. To annoy them he used to call them when he woke up, but he had long given that up. He now wrote music in the mornings after taking the children to school. It suited him. Solveig worked for a new travel agency that was expanding rapidly.

They drank their coffee. David looked at the paper Stefan had put on the table between them but didn't open it. There was a picture of a car crash on the front page and a story about the passengers.

"David," said Stefan, leaning over the table, "I . . ."

David wasn't ready for this conversation yet so he waved to the waiter.

"I'd like another coffee, please," he said.

Stefan stretched and shot another glance at the young woman by the window. She sensed he was watching her and looked up.

"Perhaps I'll have a beer," said Stefan.

They waited for the waiter in silence. Stefan tapped his fingers on the table.

"I haven't seen you up at the stables," he commented.

"I've been going at a different time," said David.

"That's what I thought," said Stefan, then added: "Where's that damn waiter?"

They were good riders. Stefan's father was well known in the business and had bought his son his first horse when he was a boy. David had started later and his horse was nowhere near the quality of Stefan's. Not to imply that Red was some kind of old hack; on the contrary, he was a fine horse, though no longer young. But Star was a prize-winning animal. Stefan's parents had given her to him for his thirtieth birthday.

They generally went to the stables together after they woke up. There were few people around at that time; most rode before work in the mornings or after work in the evenings. Their horses were stabled opposite each other with a paddock in between where they could exercise. They bought lunch on their way to the stables, usually a hamburger, sometimes Chinese. But after Ester moved in with David he had started to eat lunch with her if she was home at midday.

She was younger than he, just turned thirty. She had studied drama, and although she didn't have a regular job she was good at picking up work. She gave courses, acted in commercials and performed in whatever shows came her way. If times were tough and she needed money she would temp at her father's company. He was a wholesaler. She had been in a beauty contest in her teens and although she hadn't won she felt she was still paying the price. In fact she was sure some of the theater crowd regarded her as a debutante. The women, especially.

She and David had met at a party more than a year ago. Their courtship had been stormy. David hadn't been prepared to commit and had continued to accept other offers that came along. Gradually, however, their relationship firmed up, and before David knew what was happening she had moved in with him. Since then he had strayed only once. She had found out, and his next few days had been hell. He confided in Stefan about his troubles, and Stefan suggested he use the opportunity to end the relationship or let her end it. David thought about it but couldn't do it. He was surprised to discover that he needed her.

She was a partier like him, and on weekends they sometimes lay in bed half the day recovering from the night before. They lived on the top floor of a little corrugated-iron house in the old town, along with Ester's cat, which she had brought with her when she moved in. An old woman lived on the floor below. When it rained they could hear the drops pattering on the skylight, which had a tendency to leak. When this happened he put a bucket in the middle of the floor and listened to the raindrops plinking inside.

David was thinking about their bed against the wall under the eaves when the waiter brought Stefan his beer. It was a double bed he had bought long ago. When he lay on his back and turned his head to the left he could see through the skylight. Sometimes he saw the moon. Not often, but it struck him as being extraordinary every time.

"Maybe I'll have a beer too," he said to the waiter. "Beer and a schnapps."

"Single?" asked the waiter.

He nodded. "Single."

They drank their beer and Stefan ordered schnapps like David. When the young woman by the window stood up they both watched her walk out. The traffic had quieted; it was nearly seven. The radio was on in the back room, and the sound of the news carried to them whenever there was a lull in the music from the CD. The local Frank Sinatra was singing in caressing tones.

"Well," said Stefan. "I never thought we'd find ourselves in a situation like this."

David pushed away his empty schnapps glass and reached for the beer.

"A situation like what?" he asked.

"I don't know what I was doing. You mustn't think that . . ."

"I'm hungry," said David.

He called the waiter and asked if it would be possible to have something to eat. The waiter said the café served bar snacks, and fetching a small menu placed it on the table between them. He could recommend the fish soup, he said. It was filling.

"Shall we have some soup?" suggested Stefan.

"I'll have soup and canapés, thanks," said David.

"Are the canapés any good?" asked Stefan.

The waiter nodded and said he could recommend the canapés.

They ordered another beer. David went to the men's room. As he washed his hands he examined himself in the mirror. He was beginning to feel the effects of the alcohol and realized as he looked in the mirror that his mood had deteriorated.

"Can't you change the music?" he asked the waiter when he sat down.

"Sure," said the waiter, "of course. What about Björk?"

"No," said David.

"For God's sake, not Björk," said Stefan. "Don't you have anything else?"

The waiter went and changed the CD.

"Johnny Cash," said Stefan.

"I'm not deaf," said David.

The waiter brought their soup and laid the cutlery on the table wrapped in thin paper napkins.

They ate their soup. A group of foreigners came in; they called to the waiter, who let them move two tables together by the window. They took off their outdoor gear before sitting down.

"I thought they'd all gone," said Stefan. "I thought they all left in the autumn."

David didn't answer. He was thinking about his bed under the eaves. It wasn't really his bed anymore. It was now his and Ester's. In fact, since his birthday it had been her bed. He hadn't slept there since.

"Which side did you do it on?" he asked.

Stefan looked up.

"What do you mean?"

"Did you do it on her side or my side of the bed?"

"Come on. It wasn't like that."

"Didn't you use the bed?"

"David, please. I thought you were here to make peace."

He had celebrated his birthday at a little restaurant where they sometimes performed. There were thirty people at the party, in a private room. It had been a happy occasion with lots of toasts and singing. For most of the evening the restaurant had been quiet, but after midnight it began to fill up. The birthday guests had all emerged and started mingling with the other customers. Ester was in high spirits, dancing on a table with David's cousin and showing off. Meanwhile David stayed at the bar, chatting to friends and acquaintances. At two in the morning a woman he knew came in. It was the woman he had slept with after Ester had moved in with him. She spotted him and smiled. They talked. Someone told her it was his birthday and she kissed him on the cheek and said: "Happy birthday." They danced together briefly, then she kissed him on the cheek again, repeating: "Happy birthday."

That was all. He went back to the bar and she disappeared. He hadn't seen Ester while he was dancing, but now his cousin came over and told him that she had rushed out.

"Where did she go?" he asked.

His cousin didn't know.

"She was mad," he said.

David shook his head. Benedikt and Solveig came to say good-bye and thank him for the evening.

"Do you think Ester has gone home?" asked Solveig. "Don't you think you should go after her?"

"I haven't a clue where she's gone," he said. "I can't go chasing after her all over town."

It was noisy and hard to talk, so Benedikt and Solveig said their good-byes and left. Stefan came over and asked if they should play something.

"All we need's a guitar," he said.

"I'll go home and get it," said David.

Stefan thought that was a good idea, but David didn't leave. He was talking and laughing and didn't feel any urgency. But Stefan really wanted to play. After having nudged David unsuccessfully a couple of times he gave up and decided to go himself.

"Give me your keys," he said. "I'll go get the guitar since you're not moving your ass."

David and Ester lived only a few minutes from the restaurant. Stefan left and David carried on partying. He had lost track of time, but after a while he began to wonder why Stefan hadn't come back. He now had the urge to play, and he assumed that Stefan had met someone and been delayed. He decided to go home and pick up not only his guitar but his bass as well. He asked his cousin to join him and they strode off, a little drunk.

Stefan came running down the stairs the moment David opened the front door. His shirt was half-buttoned and he was try-ing to tuck it into his pants and pull on his jacket at the same time. David knew instantly what had happened, and Stefan saw it in his face.

"Look, don't misunderstand this," Stefan said, but didn't get any further because David went for him. They collapsed on the floor by the front door, David beating Stefan until his cousin separated them. The fight was accompanied by crashes and yells that woke the old woman downstairs. She opened the door but shut it again immediately. By then Stefan had fled the scene and David was beside himself.

"You bastard," he said, "you fucking bastard . . ."

Ester had appeared at the top of the stairs. She was crying, and for an instant her eyes met David's. Then he rushed out, and she ran down the stairs and outside after him, shrieking between her sobs: "David, David . . . !" raising her voice on the last syllable. But he was gone and his cousin led her back inside and told her to go to bed.

Since then Ester and David had not spoken. She had tried in vain to get hold of him, but as soon as he heard her voice on his phone he hung up. He had gone straight to Benedikt and Solveig's place. They had sat with him in the kitchen till morning, when he finally agreed to crawl into bed. He had been staying with them ever since because he didn't want his parents to find out what was going on. They might not hear anything, but other people soon would because word got around. David couldn't get over it, and Benedikt sat with him for hours, trying to convince him that it wasn't the end of the world. For a while Benedikt made no progress, but eventually he persuaded David to meet Stefan. He had told David repeatedly that Stefan was so upset he couldn't sleep.

"It was the booze," said Benedikt. "You both drink too much. He would never have done this sober."

They finished their soup and the waiter took away the bowls.

"You know I'd never have done it sober," said Stefan. "I don't really remember anything."

"Which side were you on?"

"What does it matter?"

"It matters to me."

David had raised his voice, and the foreigners looked in their direction.

"We've been friends for almost twenty years," said Stefan. "I wish it had never happened. It was the biggest mistake I've ever made in my life."

"Fifteen years," corrected David. "We've only known each other fifteen years."

The waiter brought the canapés. David ordered another beer. Stefan followed suit. The canapés were disappointing.

David had been waking up at the same time as Benedikt and his family since he had moved in with them, so he had started going to the stables when Benedikt took the kids to school. He knew he wouldn't be in any danger of meeting Stefan at that hour, and anyway he enjoyed starting the day with his horse. He had always trusted him and knew that the horse felt the same way. He met riders he had never seen before, and they asked if he was new. He said he'd been coming to the stables for years but usually rode at a different time. Someone recognized him and said: "Of course you must work nights a lot."

Most mornings he looked in on Star. She knew him and always seemed pleased to see him. He told himself that he wasn't going to make her suffer for Stefan's shortcomings. Generally he slipped her either a bit of hay or a slice of rye bread. She was good-natured and had always taken care to allow Red to keep up with her when he and Stefan were riding out together. It was as if she didn't want to humiliate old Red.

Once Ester came to the stables. She had called Benedikt and he told her where David was. She pulled up in her father's car and parked beside David. He was finishing up when she arrived and didn't notice her until she was standing in front of the stables. She looked at him nervously, waiting for him to say something. But he said nothing, just stared at her, picturing her with Stefan. Then he walked straight past her, got in his car and drove away.

They ordered schnapps when they had finished the canapés. The place was beginning to fill up, and the customers' voices merged with the music. Stefan stared into his glass, saying: "Fifteen years, David. You've been my best friend for fifteen years. Do you think you can forgive me?"

David stared into space for a while, then looked up.

"I don't know," he said. "I don't know if I can forgive you."

He felt almost sad as he said this, and Stefan was so overcome that he wiped his eyes. They knew how to be silent in each other's company, had done so for years in buses, taxis and planes. Now they were silent at the table, and it felt no worse than talking. Neither of them had drunk much since the birthday party, David adjusting to Benedikt's family lifestyle, Stefan blaming alcohol for what had happened and considering giving up drinking altogether. But now there was nothing to be done but order another beer and another schnapps and hope that the drinks would combine to anesthetize their misery.

A man they knew came in and took a seat with them. He was funny and they laughed at his stories. When he got up and went to join the people he had come in with, they paid the bill and left.

The weather had turned cold; the forecast was for frost. It was nearing midnight and neither wanted to go home. Stefan suggested visiting a bar around the corner and having a nightcap. David couldn't see anything wrong with that; he couldn't ignore the fact that he was fond of Stefan and had missed him since his birthday. That's what he found strangest. That he felt a sense of loss when he should have been seething with rage. It bothered him because he felt that somehow it wasn't right that he didn't hate Stefan for what he had done. It actually seemed wrong. But he couldn't help it, had no control over it. At the same time he doubted he could ever forgive him. He had no power over that either.

The bar was packed. They recognized some of the customers but didn't talk to them. They carried on drinking and began to reminisce about old times. Alcohol made them sentimental, and both were affected by the temporary sincerity that drink brings. Yet they didn't mention Ester, not until the middle of the night when Stefan asked David again whether he could forgive him. David answered as before and then Stefan asked if he could forgive Ester. David said he didn't know if he could.

"Please, David, she's a good girl. It was all my fault. Hate me but forgive her."

"I don't hate you," David said. "I've never hated you."

"You can hate me," Stefan said. "I deserve it. But you can't hate Ester. She's a good girl. It was all my fault."

"I don't hate you," David said.

"But you should," Stefan said. "You should hate me. But not Ester. You shouldn't hate her."

The following day David couldn't remember how the conversation had turned to the horses. Not exactly. The word "compensation" was never used, though afterward it cropped up more than once in David's thoughts. It was not the only word that came to mind, but the other words were not to his liking, so he tried to ignore them.

"You can trust them," he remembered Stefan saying. "Red and Star. You can always trust them."

"Red's getting old," David said. "Last night I dreamed I'd lost him. Both him and Ester. I dreamed that I was alone."

"It's all my fault," said Stefan.

"He's getting old."

"I'll give you Star," Stefan said. "I want you to have her."

David objected, but not forcefully. Before he knew it not only had they shaken hands on it but Stefan had actually confirmed it in writing on a small paper napkin that the bartender gave him.

They hugged outside the bar and David stuck the napkin in his pocket. There was a pale moon in the east, a few harmless wisps of cloud drifting across it from time to time. The temperature had dropped.

"Do you think you can ever forgive me?" asked Stefan in parting.

David said he already had.

Stefan took a taxi, but David decided to walk home to Benedikt's. He reached into his pocket for the napkin and examined it for a while in the light from a lamppost before taking out his wallet and putting it inside beside two thousand-krona bills. He thought about Star, her fluid movements, her willingness and stamina, and about the prizes Stefan had accumulated over the years. And he thought about Ester and their bed by the wall under the eaves.

He had nearly reached Benedikt's house when, unable to resist the impulse, he hailed a passing taxi. He only realized how tired he was when he took a seat in the back; his eyelids drooped from time to time during the journey, but he wouldn't turn back because he had to see her. When they reached their destination the driver nudged him. David started but managed to climb out of the car unaided.

"Are you sure you don't want me to wait for you?" asked the driver.

David said there was no need.

She was asleep. He moved carefully so as not to wake her, but she stirred anyway, scrambled up and shook herself. She knew him at once. As he patted her, she looked at him with her soft eyes, and he realized all of a sudden that Stefan had betrayed her by giving her away. As he himself had betrayed Red, who had been like a brother to him all these years. That was the word he used as he stood there in the stable: "brother." When he reached the point of blaming himself for swapping Ester for a horse, he wept.

Star watched him leave. He closed the door behind him, the tears streaming down his cheeks. He reached into his wallet for the napkin, scrunched it up and threw it in the dirt.

He vaguely remembered the napkin when he woke up. It was close to noon and had started to rain. The hay was soft and the smell of Red reminded him where he was. He didn't open his eyes at once but listened to the rain on the roof. He pictured the skylight in his apartment and the moon that had appeared to him from time to time as he lay in his bed under the eaves.

november

Richard stood in the rain outside the hospital, waiting for their daughter, June. He didn't want to wait inside; he couldn't bear the smell or the thought of death. He wished he had been injured too, but he hadn't been so lucky. The car had hit the passenger side. His shoulder and neck were a little tender from the seatbelt, but that was all. He had felt as if the nursing staff were looking at him accusingly after they examined him. He knew it was all in his mind, but the feeling was there anyway. By then Kathryn was already on the operating table.

He and Kathryn would meet at June's house on birthdays and holidays. She had never needed to worry about inviting them together because they were always perfectly civilized to each other and everyone else. They often sat side by side at the table, their behavior unstrained, and there was never any echo of the past in their conversations. It had long ago become customary for him to drive Kathryn home after the parties since it was on his way and there was no need to put June or Don to the trouble. They were busy enough cleaning up. Kathryn lived in a one-bedroom apartment by the sea, he in a one-bedroom apartment on the west side of town. At times he would avoid shortcuts to her home because he was not at all averse to having her in the car. Their town was just north of Boston. You could see the city from the hills close to June's house.

The divorce had been unavoidable, and no one's fault but his own. Kathryn had put up with his drinking longer than he deserved, nursing him and helping him cover up the illness. At the time they married he would drink no more than was commonplace in those years, and then mostly on weekends when they went out on the town or to parties at friends' houses. But over the years his drinking escalated; the weekend extended, became a week, two weeks, a month.

He went to rehab in Maine. It hadn't been easy to get in there, but family and colleagues had written testimonies on his behalf and his Rotary friends had provided financial support. Richard worked as a lawyer in the public sector and his bosses were understanding. When he came home he talked like a born-again Christian. Even Kathryn, who had seen it all before and didn't believe in miracles, felt convinced that this time it was real. As expected, she was vigilant the first few months, but he was so determined and candid that gradually she relaxed. They started going to the theater again and for walks in the nature reserves outside of town or down by the sea; he talked of making up to her and June for the past and said a lot of nice things to her that stayed in her memory.

It was a crushing blow when he relapsed. He had been drinking in secret for some time, and Kathryn asked herself how she could have failed to know that. He promised repeatedly to stop but never managed to stay dry for long.

He could not deceive Kathryn again. She seemed to have a sixth sense for what was going to happen, like weather-wise people who can detect storms long in advance. In the end she gave up and they divorced. June was in her teens by then. Of course she was upset but she was old enough to understand. She and her mother were very close and made each other happy. Their relationship was what made life bearable for them both.

Richard lost his job. For several years he was so far gone that sometimes months would pass without his being in a fit state to visit his daughter, who could hardly recognize him as the same man. Later he moved to Boston and took up with a woman who was as hard-living as he was. He so completely vanished from view that mother and daughter began to refer to him in the past tense. Kathryn was now working full-time at the local energy company, and June was doing well in high school. On the rare occasions when Richard's name came up in conversation Kathryn was careful not to speak ill of him.

He stopped drinking when his health could no longer stand it. He was admitted to the hospital, and the doctors discovered that the damage extended beyond his liver and kidneys to his heart. Kathryn and June visited him, prepared for him to die any minute. But slowly he recovered and was back on his feet within a few weeks. After spending six months in various institutions, he rented an apartment and even got a position at the Inland Revenue thanks to one of his Rotary friends. When June graduated from university shortly afterward he was the first person to turn up at Kathryn's house for the party. He brought her the complete *Oxford English Dictionary* as a present, and although he didn't speak much one found his presence uncomfortable.

This evening they had been celebrating the eighth birthday of June and Don's daughter, little Kate. Her friends had been invited during the day and grown-ups in the evening, after the little girls had eaten their pizza and cake and gone home. Don's parents and siblings were there as well as Richard and Kathryn. June had baked two cakes, one chocolate, one fruit, and they had coffee with the cakes and talked about the sorts of things people talk about on such occasions. Little Kate was tired, and her behavior began to deteriorate toward ten, so Richard took her into her bedroom and read her a book she had been given for her birthday. She fell asleep quickly, and he sat with her for a while after she dropped off. It had begun to rain and gust, so before he left her he closed the window and popped a couple of menthol sweets in his mouth.

It was nearly eleven by the time he and Kathryn left. They would have left earlier if it hadn't been a Friday evening. Don's siblings stayed on; they were going to play cards once June and Don had cleaned up. Unable to find a parking space outside the house, Richard had parked farther down the street. He told Kathryn to wait in the hall while he went out in the rain to fetch the car. He returned after a little while, opened the door for her and switched on the windshield wipers. It was pouring.

This evening he decided not to take the long way to her home. They stopped at a red light soon after they set off, and Richard used the opportunity to wipe the condensation off the windows.

"The little girl's growing up," he said.

"Yes, she certainly is."

"She takes after her mother."

"In many ways. But after her father too."

"Yes, but more after her mother. Always on the go."

"She's a clever little thing."

There were not many cars on the road, but he drove carefully in the rain. He was always accustomed to driving slowly, keeping to the right on highways so that other cars could pass easily. He had bought the car used. It was Japanese and reliable. He had taken it in for tuning a week ago and would soon change over to winter tires. It was November, but there had not been any snow yet.

"It's really coming down," he said.

"It's supposed to rain all weekend," she replied.

"Our June is a fine girl," he said. "A real hard worker. She gets that from you."

"It's always a pleasure to visit them," she said. "And Don pulls his weight."

"Yes, she's lucky with Don. And little Kate. Do you think there's any chance of them having another before long?"

"Who knows," she said. "They're both so busy. June has just got that promotion and Don's always traveling. Did you hear that he has to spend two weeks in Oregon before Christmas?"

"No," he said. "I didn't hear that. I was probably reading to Kate. Two weeks?"

"Yes, that's what he said. He's so good with people. I expect that's why they send him rather than someone else."

"Yes," he said. "I expect that's why. But I do hope they have another one soon. They're such good parents."

When they reached the hill leading down to the ocean he slowed down still further. He could hardly see a thing for all the rain, and there was fog on the inside of the windows again. He held the wheel with his left hand and wiped the condensation with his right.

"Did little Kate take a long time to settle?" she asked.

"No," he said. "I read to her a little, then she was out. Exhausted after the day."

"But you spent at least half an hour in there with her."

"Did I? Yes, I suppose so. I wanted to make sure she was asleep before I left her. She sleeps peacefully. I was thinking about her mother when she was a girl."

They saw the city in the distance. It was black in the rain, and its lights seemed to be struggling to pierce the darkness. He turned up the heat on the windshield and opened his window a crack to try to get rid of the condensation. He could see better now than before. He reflected on how much the city had changed since he was a boy growing up there.

"It'll be Christmas before you know it," he said. "We can do with the lights during these short, dark days. But you've never minded them, have you?"

She adjusted the bag on her lap without answering.

"Richard," she said after a pause, "have you started drinking again?"

He flinched.

"What on earth makes you think that?"

She had been looking straight ahead when she asked him, but now she turned and studied him for a while.

"You've started drinking again."

He didn't try to lie to her. He knew he couldn't. Instead he berated himself for having gone to the party. It had been a big mistake. He should have known she'd see through him.

"I could tell you'd been drinking when you arrived," she said, "and after you'd been in with Kate. Did you have a miniature in your pocket?"

He was silent, concentrating on driving.

"I haven't started drinking," he said at last. "Not like before. I take a nip every now and then. For my circulation. You mustn't misunderstand it."

"You're driving drunk," she said.

"I'm not drunk," he said. "How can you say that?"

"And you had another drink when you went to get the car. Have you got more alcohol in the glove compartment?"

"It's not like you think. I've been doing well. It's six years since I quit. Kate was only two. She's never seen me drunk."

"Not until this evening."

"Don't tell them. Don't do that to me, Kathryn. I'll never let it happen again."

She adjusted the bag on her lap again. Shifted it, then opened it to take out a handkerchief. She had her hand in the bag when the accident happened.

Richard drove through a red light. He hadn't been aware of the lights, hadn't been aware of anything but the fear in his own breast. Perhaps his eyes had been on the glove compartment, perhaps on her as she reached in her bag for the handkerchief. He had driven straight in front of a brand-new Jeep. The eighteen-year-old driver had borrowed it from his parents and was on his way home from the movies. He smelled of cigarette smoke, but the police didn't know whether he had been drinking. They informed Richard of that when they arrived at the hospital. They said they didn't know whether the boy had been drinking but mentioned that they would be doing a blood test on him. The boy was on the operating table like Kathryn, but his injuries were not considered serious.

Her condition was another matter. The Jeep had hit her side of the car at full speed, and she had to be removed through the driver's door. She was unconscious, the blood streaming down her face. Richard didn't have a cell phone and doubted anyway whether he would have had the strength to call an ambulance. A taxi driver who arrived on the scene immediately after the accident had reported it. At that point Richard was still sitting in the car and hadn't even tried to move. He was hoping he wouldn't be able to.

He managed to remove the flask from the glove compartment before the police and ambulance arrived. Seizing the chance while the taxi driver was tending to the boy in the Jeep, he dropped the flask in the weeds beside the road.

He waited in the hospital corridor after they had examined him. A nurse asked whether she should contact relatives, but he said no thank you, he would do it himself. She offered him the use of the phone in reception, so he got up and walked slowly over. It was nearly midnight. The phone was white.

Now he was standing outside in the rain, waiting. Kathryn's condition was critical, and the doctors couldn't say for sure how long the operation would take. The wind tore at the flagpole on the lawn outside while the trees along the road swayed back and forth.

A car turned into the parking lot and stopped by the maternity unit. A young man helped a pregnant woman climb out.

He didn't know if he wanted Kathryn to live. When he realized this he felt so terrible that his stomach turned. He tried to ward off the thought, tried to silence the voice that was saying: "If she lives she'll tell June everything. If she dies no one will know."

He stood waiting in the rain. The wind grew stronger. His thoughts went to the flask that he had left by the side of the road. It was still more than half full.

december

The old friends used to meet at Joe and Debbie's place between Christmas and New Year's, usually on the twenty-eighth or twenty-ninth. They ate dinner together and always meant to play cards afterward but never did. Instead they talked, drank wine and sang. Henry had given up drinking but he joined in the singing and was sure he enjoyed himself just as much as the others. He had quit a few years back but still attended AA meetings every Saturday morning in a church not far from the sea. The meetings lasted an hour, and when they were over he would remind himself how lucky he was. He was an engineer, and he and his wife were comfortably off; Fay had gone back to her job as a lab technician when their two older boys started university. Their youngest was in middle school. He was little trouble, spending most of his time on the computer. They had a marriage others envied.

The party went on late as a rule, but since Henry had gone on the wagon he and Fay tended to leave before one. Nobody complained, though Henry knew that after they had gone his friends would make good-natured fun of him for having given up drinking. Maybe they would also reminisce about old incidents from previous Christmas reunions, such as the time he went out to fight the snowman in the garden. He didn't remember it himself, but Fay had described the fight to him in detail when he woke up the next day. He gathered that the snowman had had the upper hand.

Fay never complained about his wanting to go home before the others. She understood that it could be difficult to be sober as the party progressed and his friends started repeating the stories they'd told earlier in the evening or some of the old stories they'd told one another countless times. That evening he had begun to give her the signal earlier than usual because it was snowing heavily outside and he was looking forward to driving home in his new Jeep. He had taken possession of it two days before Christmas, and this was the first time it had snowed since then. He had watched the snow falling as they ate and hoped that only the main roads would be plowed before morning.

Debbie stood in the hall with Fay while he scraped the snow off the car. Joe put his boots on and came out to join him. He walked around the car, suggesting Henry should get himself bigger tires. Henry found this absurd but didn't say anything because he didn't want to hurt Joe, who had had his own Jeep jacked up. Fay hadn't brought along any outdoor shoes so they helped her to the car.

"I'll have to clear the path before I go to bed," said Joe.

He and Debbie waved them off as they drove away.

The car smelled of leather. Henry breathed it in. Fay had drunk her share of white wine and a little bit of red, and she snuggled up against him. He had watched her during the evening when she wasn't paying attention. She always looked beautiful to him, and when she smiled he couldn't help smiling to himself.

"I think my feet got wet on the way to the car," she said, letting her high heels fall on the floor and tucking her feet under her. "I didn't know it was going to snow."

"The car will warm up quickly," he said. "You'll be dry soon."

He pushed a button on the dashboard to increase the blast. She curled up on the seat and pressed herself closer to him. He felt no less fond of her now than when they had first met twenty-four years ago. Her hair touched his cheek and though it tickled he didn't pull away.

"They told me she performs well in snow," he said. "She holds the road well."

"Will's going skiing tomorrow," she said. "I'd better make some sandwiches for him when we get home so I don't have to do it in the morning."

"I'll do it," he said. "I haven't had a chance to try the four-wheel drive yet, so I'll give him a lift tomorrow. I'll make his sandwiches before we go."

"Thanks, love," she said, then turned on the radio, switching from station to station before turning it off again.

"Why can't they play something for us?" she said. "It's the same songs on every station."

"People our age should be in bed," he said. "They're only playing music for teenagers now."

She smiled. "People our age . . . Think how old we're getting. Joe's fifty."

"Yes, but he's older than us."

"Only two years older than you."

Her voice held a teasing note. They both smiled.

The city slumbered under its white pelt. The old lighthouse flashed its white beam into the darkness, perhaps more from habit than necessity, tonight at any rate. Henry felt a great fondness for this modest New England town where he and his friends had lived their whole lives. He had missed it when he was studying in California. He drove slowly, relishing the journey.

"I'm the youngest in the group, aren't I?" she said.

"Are you sure?"

"What do you mean by that?" she asked, elbowing him. "As if you didn't know."

"Maybe I'm so old I've forgotten. Not by much, anyway."

He smiled. She smiled back.

"Not by much . . ." she repeated.

It was warm in the car so he turned down the heater.

"Are your feet still wet?"

"Feel for yourself."

"I can't reach."

"Stretch. Then you'll be able to."

"Then I'll go off the road and end up in a snowdrift."

"Why not? We could keep each other warm. Remember?"

"That was a long time ago."

"It was snowing like now. It didn't take you long to park the car by the lighthouse when we got down to the cove. It's not far from here. . . ."

"Are you sure you didn't have too much wine?"

"Are you too old for it?"

"We're both too old for it."

"I'm not."

She kissed him on the earlobe and whispered: "I don't think you're too old either."

"At least I'm not bald like Michael."

"Poor Michael," she said.

"Or Johnson," he added. "Both bald as coots."

"You and Joe still have your hair."

"Yes, I should probably be grateful I'm only going gray."

They drove past the lake where their boys used to go skating when they were younger. The branches of the trees were bowed under the weight of the snow. The temperature was just below freezing. The snow was wet, but the Jeep held the road well. Henry swapped lanes for no reason, just to see if the Jeep would skid.

"Henry," she said.

"Mm?" he replied absentmindedly.

"You want me to tell you a secret?"

"Yes, tell me a secret."

"No, it's not a good idea."

"Why not?"

"Just because."

She snuggled up to him again.

"Aren't you looking forward to coming home with me?"

"I'm sure Will's awake," he said.

"He was going to stay with Alex. Don't you remember? They're going skiing together tomorrow."

"Oh yes, I forgot Alex was going with him."

"We'll be alone together."

He changed lanes again.

"Aren't you looking forward to going to bed with a younger woman?"

"Not unless you tell me your secret."

"No, I don't want to."

"Oh?"

"You might get angry."

"I never get angry."

"Do you promise?"

"How much did you have to drink, anyway?"

"Do you promise?"

"On my mother's grave."

She kissed him on the cheek and neck before whispering: "Sometimes when we're making love I imagine I'm with someone else. Sometimes it's Joe."

He felt a sharp pain in his stomach and his palms were sweaty, but he tried not to show it.

"Why?"

"Are you angry?"

"No."

"I shouldn't have told you."

He stopped at a light. It was red for a long time.

"Often?"

"No, not often at all."

"Why?"

"I don't know. A fantasy. Don't you ever fantasize like that?"

"No."

"I shouldn't have told you. Now I feel guilty."

He stared at the light till it turned green. He didn't know how he felt. Couldn't figure it out.

"Are you looking forward to coming to bed with me?"

He pulled her against him. He was looking forward to it, though he didn't say anything.

After she had fallen asleep he went into the living room. He sat in a chair by the window but didn't turn on the light. The snow lit up the room. He was sweaty from their lovemaking and had put on a bathrobe so he wouldn't catch a chill. The snow had stopped falling, and the moon was shining on the white garden.

It had been good. It was always good, but this time it had been unusually good. While they were making love he had been thinking about what she had told him, and he asked her whether she was fantasizing about anyone as she wrapped herself around him.

"What are you thinking about?" he had whispered.

"Nothing," she had whispered back.

"Are you sure?"

"Do you want me to think about Joe? Is that what you want?"

It had been unusually good, but now the excitement had ebbed from his body and been replaced by uncertainty, fear and an odd sadness. He knew he would not be able to look at Joe the same way the next time they met. Perhaps he would never be able to look at him the same way. Yet Joe had done nothing wrong, never been anything but his most loyal friend.

He stared out into the garden, trying to reason with himself because he didn't like the way his thoughts were tending. He had begun to blame Fay, to persuade himself that she had cheated on him. He was a reasonable, sensible man by nature and usually kept his head when things went wrong, but now he was afraid that he was losing his sensibility. He recalled past events and accused himself of hypocrisy. All Fay had done was allow her thoughts to stray. Was that so terrible? Had it harmed him in any way? Hadn't he indirectly encouraged her to fantasize about Joe when they got home tonight?

He sat by the window till morning. Then he went into the kitchen and made sandwiches for Will before going down to the storeroom to fetch his skis and skiwear. He carried them to the hall, then put on his boots and got the car keys and his wallet from the coat he had been wearing when they had visited Joe and Debbie. There would be few people on the road, and he tried to discipline his thoughts, think about the journey to the mountains, the highway, the turnoff, the white slopes at their destination, the fresh mountain air.

He had put on his jacket and was about to open the front door when he paused. His fingers were clenched on the car keys, and he loosened his grip as he walked slowly back into the house. He had turned off the lights on his way out but didn't bother to turn them on again. His eyes grew accustomed to the darkness, and when he reached the bedroom he pushed the door gently open, stopped on the threshold and let his arms drop to his sides.

Fay was asleep. Her breathing was slow and regular where his was rapid, so he waited a little until he had calmed down. Then he cleared his throat and announced into the silence: "I slept with Debbie."

Fay didn't stir. The red Christmas lights in the tree outside shone through the curtains, casting a faint glow on the bed. She seemed peaceful, and although she wasn't smiling, it looked as if she were having a pleasant dream.

"I slept with Debbie," he repeated, adding: "Twice. I was drunk."

Fay didn't wake up, though she did turn over and mutter something in her sleep.

He waited a while, then closed the door again. He took the skis, the packed lunch and the skiwear and went out. It had started snowing again. Everything was white. He sat in the car for a long time before finally driving off.

ALSO BY OLAF OLAFSSON

ABSOLUTION

In his spellbinding first novel, Olaf Olafsson takes us inside the haunted mind of expatriate businessman Peter Peterson who left behind a secret that shadowed his accomplishments and estranged him from his loved ones—a crime of passion, committed in the throes of unrequited love, that became a lifetime's burden. Yet when Peter is forced to confront the consequences of his actions, an unexpected turn of events shakes the very foundations of his past.

Fiction/Literature/978-1-4000-3068-2

THE JOURNEY HOME

In this lyrical and arresting novel, Olaf Olafsson tells the story of Disa Jonsdottir's redemptive journey back to Iceland. Along the way memories surface—of the silence between her and her mother, of the fate of her German-Jewish lover, of the pivotal encounter she had while working as a cook in a wealthy household. Skillfully weaving past and present, Olafsson captures the full range of Disa's experiences, ultimately building toward an emotional climax that renders *The Journey Home* moving and unforgettable.

Fiction/Literature/978-0-385-72041-0

WALKING INTO THE NIGHT

As butler to William Randolph Hearst, Christian Benediktsson lives quietly, almost invisibly. It is in his thoughts and in unsent letters to his wife back in Iceland that we witness the unraveling of his former life, which began when he abandoned his family for an actress in New York City. Once a successful businessman, he erases his past after a sudden tragic death and his financial ruin, the result of a jilted lover's vengeance. *Walking into the Night* is a stunning portrait of a man wrestling with guilt and secret passions.

Fiction/Literature/978-1-4000-3480-2

ANCHOR BOOKS
Available at your local bookstore, or visit www.randomhouse.com